GIRL DECEIVED

Girl Missing

Book 6

KATE GABLE

KATE GABLE

Copyright

Proofreaders:

Julie Deaton, Deaton Author Services, https://www.facebook.com/jdproofs/

Renee Waring, Guardian Proofreading Services, https://www.facebook.com/GuardianProofreadingServices

Cover Design: Kate Gable

Visit my website at www.kategable.com

Be the first to know about my upcoming sales, new releases and exclusive giveaways!

Want a Free book? Sign up for my Newsletter!

Sign up for my newsletter:
https://www.subscribepage.com/kategableviplist

Join my Facebook Group: https://www.facebook.com/groups/833851020557518

Bonus Points: Follow me on BookBub and Goodreads!

https://www.goodreads.com/author/show/21534224.Kate_Gable

About Kate Gable

Kate Gable loves a good mystery that is full of suspense. She grew up devouring psychological thrillers and crime novels as well as movies, tv shows and true crime.

Her favorite stories are the ones that are centered on families with lots of secrets and lies as well as many twists and turns. Her novels have elements of psychological suspense, thriller, mystery and romance.

Kate Gable lives near Palm Springs, CA with her husband, son, a dog and a cat. She has spent more than twenty years in Southern California and finds inspiration from its cities, canyons, deserts, and small mountain towns.

She graduated from University of Southern California with a Bachelor's degree in Mathematics. After pursuing graduate studies in mathematics, she switched gears and got her MA in Creative Writing and English from Western New Mexico University and her PhD in Education from Old Dominion University.

Writing has always been her passion and

obsession. Kate is also a USA Today Bestselling author of romantic suspense under another pen name.

Write her here:

Kate@kategable.com

Check out her books here:

www.kategable.com

Sign up for my newsletter:
https://www.subscribepage.com/kategableviplist

Join my Facebook Group:
https://www.facebook.com/groups/833851020557518

Bonus Points: Follow me on BookBub and Goodreads!

https://www.bookbub.com/authors/kate-gable

https://www.goodreads.com/author/show/21534224.Kate_Gable

amazon.com/Kate-Gable/e/B095XFCLL7

facebook.com/kategablebooks

bookbub.com/authors/kate-gable

instagram.com/kategablebooks

Also by Kate Gable

Detective Kaitlyn Carr Psychological Mystery series

Girl Missing (Book 1)

Girl Lost (Book 2)

Girl Found (Book 3)

Girl Taken (Book 4)

Girl Forgotten (Book 5)

Girl Deceived (Book 6)

Girl Hunted (Book 7)

Girl Shadowed (Book 8)

Girl Hidden (FREE Novella)

FBI Agent Alexis Forrest Series

Forest of Silence

Forest of Shadows

Forest of Secrets

Forest of Lies
Forest of Obsession
Forest of Regrets

Detective Charlotte Pierce Psychological Mystery series
Last Breath
Nameless Girl
Missing Lives
Girl in the Lake

Lake of Lies (FREE Novella)

About Girl Deceived

A letter throws Detective Kaitlyn Carr's life into turmoil...

Settling into a new routine, Kaitlyn believes that her troubles are behind her. But then she receives a letter from a retired FBI agent, which states that everything she knows about her father's death is a lie.

The FBI agent says that her father was murdered and promises to tell her what really happened, but only if she helps him first.

To find out the truth, Kaitlyn must travel to a place with a near-constant cover of clouds and rain and investigate a series of cold cases that the

FBI agent believes are connected to the same illusive serial killer.

Here, the foliage is thick. The rains wash away evidence. It's the perfect place to bury bodies, or to leave them somewhere no one will find them.

The FBI agent might be a conspiracy theorist and Kaitlyn isn't sure if she believes any of it until she finds a young woman's body and wonders if her murder is also linked to the serial killer.

Deep in the pines and gloom of the Pacific Northwest, Kaitlyn hunts the serial killer, but what she does not yet know is that she might be the one who is being hunted....

Chapter 1

From behind the wheel of a car things somehow made sense when they previously didn't. It had been unseasonably warm, to a point where it was almost stifling, and so I just drove. I had a few days off, nothing major, nothing to look forward to, but I had some things to figure out. I was only going to drive a little bit away, just around the neighborhood, maybe on the freeway a little bit. I needed to clear my head after everything that had happened. My sister was safe and sound but to say that she was okay would be an oversimplification. She has gone through so much, and I have as well, it was hard to wrap my head around.

Then there was this letter. It came yesterday morning. In fact, it might have been dropped off a lot earlier but I don't go through the mail that often. It just piles up on the kitchen counter until I go through and throw away all the advertisements, and everything else that I don't need, leaving the envelopes to wait for a better time to be opened. That's how I missed numerous thank you notes from cases that I've worked on. That's how I missed invitations to certain events. That's how I missed this letter.

It is from a special agent with the FBI, Donald C. Clark, retired.

I didn't think much of it. It hadn't come in any special envelope, and the return address is somewhere in a city I've never heard of, but the three letters, FBI, definitely call my attention. Why would they be writing to me? Why wouldn't they call? Does it even have anything to do with them? And a retired agent? What could this be about?

It was a Tuesday morning when I opened the letter over breakfast. I sat in my dining room crowded with piles of books. It's a small, one-bedroom apartment and it should probably be a little bit better organized than it is, but I'm hardly ever home and I don't have much of a flare for interior design.

I have four big Ikea bookshelves all around overflowing with paperbacks and hardcovers mostly bought at used bookstores. The Kindle app on my phone is likewise filled to the brim but, of course, with plenty more storage. That's what I turn to when I have a little time to kill at work.

Today I pull my attention away from my favorite mystery novels. I stare at the letter once again. I hadn't bothered opening it last night, but it weighed on me so much so that it's the first thing I reached for when I grabbed my coffee.

I remember the moment as I am driving down an anonymous suburban neighborhood street with lush old trees that provide plenty of shade. I only now realize that the letter that I had received had separated my life into a before and an after. There are these pivotal moments in life where you're doing one thing that seems to change your life forever. Opening this letter was going to be one such thing.

Dear Kaitlyn,

I met you only once when you were a child. Your father had brought me to your home for dinner. I doubt that you have any memory of me but I have plenty of you, and even more of your father. He had a great, inquisitive mind, and was an even better man. People like to pay lip service to how much they love their wives and children but in your father's case, it was true.

Reading that, big tears welled up in my eyes. He had mentioned my father. A man I hadn't thought of in a very long time. Not seriously. There are the fleeting thoughts, of course. Here and there, a song that reminded me of him, a movie, a funny joke. But mostly, I tried to put all of the pain associated with his death away from me. Now, on this unassuming Tuesday morning, here it was staring me straight in the face, or more like punching me in the mouth. I take a deep breath and return to the letter. I don't want to read anymore, and yet I'm compelled to. I can't not look at it.

As I drive, the memories flood back. I remember picking up the paper, how it had been folded three times with two creases across the middle to fit into the envelope, and holding it in my hands and. The paper was stiff, brand new. The handwriting was deliberate, not rushed. Clearly enunciated. The letters themselves, almost the same height, like someone who had learned to write cursive following the dot-to-dot method. I haven't had much experience reading cursive, or any handwritten letters for that matter, but everything about Donald C. Clark's handwriting is pristine and legible. When I wipe my tears, I gather a hold of myself and look at the paper again.

My dearest Kaitlyn, I have tried to write this letter a number of times. Picked it up, threw it away. I tried to write this in an email, I tried to call, but it's the letter that I always came back to. I have worked on this version a number of times to try to make it the best that I could and yet here we are. The words are just flowing out of me as I finish my sixth beer. This is likely the one that I'm going to mail.

I don't know where to begin because there are so many

unknowns. All I want to say is that your father is not the man that you thought that he was. I'm not saying that he was a bad man, far from it, but I think he would want you to know that he did not commit suicide. He loved you very much, and he would want you to know the truth. Maybe I'm the wrong person to tell it to you, but here we are. He was murdered. He had been part of something that maybe he shouldn't have been a part of. I'm not one to judge. We all make our own mistakes and God knows I've made plenty of my own.

If you ever want to know more about this, get in touch. Don't wait too long because the cancer growing in my colon is not going to wait around forever. I'm sorry I haven't told you more and that this probably will feel like I'm baiting you to come and visit me. I am. This is a story that should be told in person, mostly because I shouldn't be telling it in the first place. I'm sorry for all the mistakes I've made, all the lies that I've told. Even if we are to never meet, I want you to know that your father was a good man. Despite everything, he loved you and he wanted what's best for you. He would be incredibly proud of the woman that you are. You have shown us all what real honor is, and that it is possible, with a little bit of gumption and effort, to actually be a decent person and a good detective. I'm just sorry that I didn't learn that lesson earlier.

I stop driving, turn right at the light, as the tears pool in my eyes. I pull over to the nearest parking lot, which is a mall with a Barnes and Noble and a Dick's Sporting Goods in front of me. I get out of the car, trying to put aside the emotions that I want nothing to do with. The letter is in my purse, and when I plunge my hand inside, I can feel it. I've read it enough to know it word for word.

What does it mean, though? What do I do with any of it? FBI Special Agent Donald C. Clark did not leave a phone number, email, or even address at the bottom of the letter. There's a return address on the envelope which, luckily, I had kept but that's all I have to go on.

Feeling uncomfortable standing in the parking lot, I go inside the mall and walk the hallways with no interest in going into any stores. But this makes me even more muddled and confused. The one thing I keep coming back to is the letter.

Chapter 2

Luke could tell that something was wrong for a while. It had been days since I'd received the letter and while, at first, I could hide it by pretending that I was busy with work, that excuse stopped working. After a little while the distance between us grew palpable. Ever since I read it, we had not done our near nightly ritual of sitting down with a few glasses of wine and watching *Hotel Hell* reruns from a decade ago, where Chef Ramsey was on TV telling all these Americans how to improve their restaurants and hotels. The predictable format, the fixer-upper nature of the show, had appealed to both of us. It was normally impossible to find a show we both liked. As close as we were, we had very little in common in terms of likes and dislikes of television and movies.

I knew tonight I couldn't pretend to do something else. When he got out two glasses of wine and asked if I wanted one, I knew that I had to tell him.

"Is something wrong?" he asked, as I searched for the right words, sticking my nose deep into the glass, trying to smell the floral notes that supposedly were there but were not exactly easy for me to find. Instead of explaining, I handed him the letter.

"This came a few days ago," I said. "Just read it, you'll know."

I watched Luke's reaction to every sentence. He was there to help me with my missing sister. Now, this new mystery had fallen in my lap, something I was completely unprepared for. On one hand, my father was already dead and so the urgency wasn't exactly there. It's something that I could let go of or take my time on.

With all these horrible thoughts making their way through my mind, I forced myself to take a sip of the wine, enjoy the moment and not eat more than five crackers as I tried to talk with the only person who would understand.

Luke is an FBI agent and has been my boyfriend for some time now. I've met his family in Kansas. He wants to take us to the next level, move from boyfriend to fiancé but due to my dysfunctional childhood and all the darkness I see at work every day, I am uncertain about having a family of my own.

"This guy knew your dad?" Luke asks looking at me through his eyelashes, scrunching up his forehead to make the little lines all too visible. He's in his mid-thirties, still as sexy and attractive as ever. Personally, probably even more so than he was in his twenties from the pictures that I've seen. He's kind, loving, understanding, and supportive. Everything that anyone could ever want. He also understands me on a level that's difficult to describe when you just know that whatever you're saying someone else is getting.

"Is this why you've been taking the car out to think so much lately?"

I shrug, "How'd you know?"

"You usually never offer to run errands; grocery store, Target."

"I know, I'm sorry." I shrug.

"No, I don't mind, you're too slow anyway," Luke says, giving me a wink.

He has a whole system, a process of when to go to what aisle to get whatever. Occasionally he'll meander. Get a few extra vegetables or frozen foods from Trader Joe's that weren't on the list, but largely, he does the shopping because he's the most efficient at it. Whenever I go there, I get lost for over an hour looking at everything.

"I figured something was wrong," Luke says,

putting the letter down, looking at me like none of this is that much of a big deal, but secretly, to me, it is. "What are you planning on doing with this? He's asking you to come up there."

"Yes, I know," I say, taking the letter from his hands and heading to the kitchen.

Our apartment is small. It's a spacious one bedroom, but it's still a one bedroom. There's a small dining room, living room, and an even smaller kitchen, but it has large windows facing Willoughby Avenue in Los Angeles. After his lease ended, Luke moved into my place because it was a little bit bigger than his even though his was newer, and now we were overflowing with stuff. Too much furniture, too many clothes, not enough space. It's not exactly the way that either of us would like it, but we're stuck with it for now.

"I think I have to go," I say.

"To Washington?"

I nod. "It just seems like something I have to do. I mean, he's dying and he's saying that he knew my father, and he wants to tell me something about him."

"He didn't give you any clues as to what he wants to tell you about him did he?"

"No, but what does that matter?"

"It matters because his intentions matter. You know that."

Luke Galvinson is a good sounding board.

He's like talking to my conscience, or rather my subconscious. Whenever I don't know which way to go, I know that he's pointing North and that he has good intentions for me regardless of where it puts him.

"I can't go with you this week; I have a big case. Last one, probably."

"What are you going to do if you quit?"

"When I quit, you mean? I don't know. Anything, everything."

I give him a slight nod. The ability to just give it all up in the middle of your career, that's not exactly something everyone can do so easily. I can't help but have doubts about him and his intentions.

"Are you trying to make me convince you to stop?" I ask.

He gives me a shrug, "No, not at all."

"Okay. Just wanted to check."

"Listen, I'm an open book. With me, what you see is what you get."

"Tell me what you see about this letter," I say. "Don't sugarcoat it."

"I think this guy is looking back on his life, thinking about any regrets he might have. I think that one of those regrets has something to do with your dad."

"I just don't know what he's going to tell me that I don't already know. I mean, I know that he was a detective and he sold drugs. He was a crooked cop, so what? I mean, it's a big deal but it's also a reality of life. The LAPD is full of them, some you can prove, some you can't. Some you just hope you never have to work with."

"That's a very jaded way of looking at it, Kaitlyn."

"I just don't see any other options," I say. "Okay, keep talking," I say after a long pause that makes me feel uncomfortable. "What else? Do you think he doesn't know that I know that my dad was crooked?"

"I have no idea. Maybe."

"Because if that's all he wants to tell me, it's probably not worth a trip."

"What if there's more?" he asks.

I shrug. I don't know where he's going with any of this. No, a more accurate description would be, I do but I don't want to think about it, and yet I can't seem to think of anything else.

The decision to go was made largely out of my control because I couldn't stop obsessing about the letter no matter what I did, and so it was better to just pull off the band-aid and head up north. I had some days off coming up, anyway.

Luke took me to the airport. It was an early morning flight and the roads were empty and slick from the unseasonable rain that had come around midnight. It was as silent and dark as a city can be, the inky blackness punctuated only by a few streetlights here and there. Both of us sat in silence and listened to a comedy podcast with three hosts who laughed uncontrollably while we just in silence without even a chuckle. It didn't necessarily mean that I didn't enjoy the podcast, it was just that I often found it difficult to laugh out loud unless the joke or the conversation was actually hilarious.

When Luke gave me a hug at Departures, I held on to him tightly. I told him that I do want to marry him and that we should do it soon. His face lit up, and I knew that his patience was growing thin. A wedding was something we hadn't really talked about. The engagement was not exactly formal, just like the way I wanted it to be. I had hoped that the wedding wouldn't be either. I didn't want to invite anybody from my department. We didn't really have any common friends. I wasn't even sure about my mom, or sister, or his family, though he wouldn't be ok with that. I don't want to be celebrated. I just want to be married, and that's it. I think Luke understands this, but I'm not sure. Not really. It's one of the few things that we haven't talked about *ad nauseum.*

Chapter 3

My flight to Seattle was uneventful. As the airplane descended through a thick blanket of clouds, I suddenly felt like I was now somewhat different after all. I rented a car and instead of heading straight to the hotel, I looked up the address on the envelope and decided to head straight down to Olympia. The capital of Washington sits about sixty miles south of Seattle, less than fifty from the airport. It should take me less than an hour with no traffic. Donald C. Clark's address was 5434 Warner Trail in Olympia, Washington. I have no meeting set up, nothing of the sort, but just like he had surprised me with the letter, I thought I would surprise him right back.

Despite being the capital, Olympia is a relatively small town with a quirky and avant-garde reputation. Evergreen College has an unusual and well-deserved reputation, with its focus on art and challenges to the status quo. This mentality seemed to spill over into the city itself. The one thing that is starkly different however is the fine line that exists between playing a hobo and actually being homeless, destitute, and a drug addict. Those two things seem to come together as one here and parts of it remind me of Skid Row back in Los Angeles.

When I get to Warner Trail though, I find Donald C. Clark's house to be pleasant, attractive, and well maintained. It's located on a quiet neighborhood street, built in the old craftsman style with a partial wrap-around porch and remodeled, shingled roof. I get to the door around one in the afternoon even though it looks more like twilight. I hadn't seen the sun all day, a little bit of brightness through the drizzle, and that's about it.

For a moment I hesitate to press the doorbell but then force myself to do it. This is an unusual time to disturb someone. Perhaps I should have called but I had no phone number.

When I ring the doorbell, a female voice yells, “Coming!"

A few minutes later a woman in her early seventies but spry and quick on her feet answers the door. She's thin, with short blonde hair and freckles all over her face, wrists, and hands. I introduce myself and before I can finish saying my name her face lights up.

"You came!" she says, introducing herself as Mary Lou Clark. "He wasn't sure if you'd be able to come and see him but, wow, I can't believe you're here. Come on in."

She ushers me inside into the warmth of the living room where the overhead lights are already lit up despite it being the middle of the day. The inside of the craftsman has tall ceilings topped with thick crown molding. Instead of the dark wood that is usually found all throughout, it has been painted in parts giving the space a brightness that it desperately needs. The windows have thick molding all around, are big and spacious with white sills but definitely original to the house. I find Mary Lou's husband, Donald, in a reclining chair in the living room with a laptop table over him.

He's lying practically all the way back and when Mary Lou announces me, he presses the button so that it slowly folds up into a sitting position.

"You're here?" he says pushing the table with the laptop away from him.

It's on little wheels and it swivels easily to the left. There's an oversized thermos cup of coffee with hot steam coming from the top next to the laptop.

Donald himself looks fit and trim given his age. He's in his mid-seventies maybe even eighty. He's got a receding hairline and a few wrinkles here and there. Lots of gray but the smile on his face is hard to deny. The orange T-shirt with jeans gives him an unusual youthful look.

"I wish you had called. I would have prepared a little better."

"I wish you'd left a phone number," I say. "Not just an address."

"Oh, that's right," he points his finger in my face.

"I told him to do it," Mary Lou pipes in, "but he said that he wanted to make sure that you would actually come by and visit and not just try to get everything out of him on the phone. He wanted to see you."

"Thanks, Mary Lou," Donald rolls his eyes and waves in her direction. It's unclear to me right now as to whether or not he can actually get up from his seat, but I decide not to press it and sit down on the couch across from him as he swivels the recliner toward me. Mary Lou offers to bring cake and cookies and tea, giving us a few moments to catch up.

"So, you worked with my father?"

"Yes, at the Big Bear Police station, for five years. I went to the FBI afterwards, decided that the local department wasn't for me."

I know there's a story there, people don't just do that, but I let it go for now.

"I'm retired from the FBI of course, worked for years, a variety of cases, some interesting some less so. Mostly out here in the Pacific Northwest."

"What brought you up here?" I asked.

"Mary Lou. Her whole family's from here. I had none to speak of, so we figured why not be next to people who love us. Plus, as you know, the Pacific Northwest has plenty of work."

"It isn't an accident they set so many murder-mystery shows in places like this."

I fill in his line of thinking. He nods. I see something in his face, a smile at the corner of the lips.

"Tell me about my father," I finally say when I get tired of dancing around the subject.

"I worked with him for five years in Big Bear. He was reliable, a good cop, trustworthy until he wasn't. All those qualities that made him a good cop is what made him a bad cop too."

"What do you mean? Like a criminal?"

"As I'm sure you know. He started taking deals, started accepting money. He wanted to do better for his family, I don't blame him but there are certain things you do and certain things you don't do. You do not become a criminal when you hunt criminals."

"My father was a complicated man," I say.

"Your father was a good man who went wrong, but we're not here to judge him. Right?"

I shrug, "Why did you write me that letter?"

"Because I wanted to see you, because I wanted to tell you some things about him that you may not know."

"Okay, I'm listening."

Mary Lou comes out placing the coffee with a tray of cookies, plates and a kettle in front of us. She makes a loud dinging sound. We work in silence for a moment, helping her arrange the snacks. I pass out plates. She sits down on the couch next to me and says, "Help yourself please."

"Mary Lou knows everything," Donald says as if I didn't already know that.

I say to myself, 'If this were Luke and me years from now, he'd know everything too.'

"I'm glad that someone knows since I'm in the dark."

Donald narrows his eyes and tilts his head to one side. He's trying to read me. The brilliant orange shirt is a little distracting, but I try to ignore it. There are bright flowers all around the house and the curtains are nice, yellow as well, probably adding some light to this darkened place. Rain starts to fall outside hitting lightly against the glass, making me feel incredibly tired.

It's not just that I was up so early, it's that I'm quite affected by the weather, the low pressure, or whatever it is that dampens the mood. Donald is buying himself some time or maybe he's just hesitating. He reaches over, grabs a scone, dips the little jam knife into the marmalade, and spreads it ever so thinly on the scone.

"My wife makes the best-baked goods."

"Yes. I can see that."

I grab one of the smaller shortcake cookies, taking a bite and letting the sugar explode in my mouth, immediately lifting my mood.

"You told me that my father did not kill himself. Is that true?"

"I don't believe that he killed himself."

This is a doubt that I've had for a long time. One that has led to arguments that have driven a wedge between my mother and me. One that is still difficult for me to grapple with.

"I've talked to one of his colleagues in Big Bear," I say. "My mother also believes that it was suicide. I just don't understand how it could not be."

"They staged it," Donald says, "He was involved with a lot of dirty people."

"Big Bear is a small mountain town. I know there are people selling drugs, but you're saying it was bigger than that?"

"Yes. They were somewhat connected to the Mexican cartel, but it went deeper. He had witnessed something. Something that had nothing to do with him being a crooked cop," Donald says taking another bite and chewing loudly. The scone makes a loud crunching sound underneath his veneers. I watch him too, as the world slows down for a moment.

"Who would want him dead?" I ask.

"It's up to you to find out the whole story," Donald says.

He takes a sip of the steaming tea and then moves to the edge of the recliner.

"He was murdered because he'd witnessed something that he shouldn't have seen. The government was involved. I know because I saw the case file with his name on it. He was listed as a witness and then he wasn't."

I narrow my eyes and move over closer to him.

"What are you talking about?"

"I'll show you the file. I'll tell you everything, but you have to promise me something. Okay? I need your help. There's a cold case that has nothing to do with your father. It's a series of missing people and I believe that they're all connected. I'm not working anymore. I'm retired and I don't have access to those materials. Not in any official capacity. I have no jurisdiction here."

"Did this happen there?"

"No," he shakes his head. "They all happened here. It's not about having jurisdiction. It's about having the ability to get around people's unwillingness to help. I'm close to finding out who's behind all of this."

"How is this related to my father?" I ask.

"It's related because if you help me, if you promise to look into it, to work the case as a private investigator, I will tell you as much as I can about what happened to your father and who killed him."

I shake my head for a moment.

"I just don't think that I can do what you want me to do."

"I think you can," he nods. "I'll show you my files. I'll show you what I have."

"Why wouldn't you use somebody in the department now? Aren't there some local police you can use?"

"People are working their own cases. They have their agendas. No one really cares about these people. Some were trafficked, some were taken, most have been gone for years. You know how it is. A new case comes in and you work that. You have 48-72 hours to solve it. If not, if you spend time working a cold case, you're not getting anywhere fast. I want to tell you about your father, everything that I know, but I need help working these first. I need someone who's experienced. I was following what happened with your sister, what you did. That takes guts. I know that you can do the same thing here."

Chapter 4

I don't waste much time telling Donald and Mary Lou that I think that they're nuts. The atmosphere is such that they seem almost amenable to it.

"I know it must sound that way," Donald says with a chuckle.

Sometimes I do find a lot of humor in these kinds of situations, but then there are other times when I just can't deal with it.

"You do realize you're saying that there's a government conspiracy that what, murdered my father?"

"Let's say that led to his murder. It's hard for me to point fingers quite yet because I don't have all the information, but once I share it with you, you will see the story is not as simple as a suicide. I know that you're going to believe me."

I finish another cookie and the sugar must be

going to my head, because all of a sudden I'm actually considering his proposal. Mary Lou pours me some more tea from the kettle. She'd steeped it on the stove and the caffeine is a little much, but it is keeping me engaged on this rainy and cloudy afternoon.

"Let's just put my father aside for a bit," I say. "Tell me about the cold cases."

"There are two missing women and a child, from different areas of the Pacific Northwest. I have a theory that it's one person."

"Is it a similar modus operandi?" I ask.

"Yes, somewhat, but he evolved his methods."

I shake my head. Donald, of all people, an FBI agent hunting serial killers for decades, should know that it's very hard to make a case that the same person was responsible for different murders in different locations.

"If the murders were not committed in the exact same way, are they similar enough?" I ask.

"I'm not going to lie to you, Kaitlyn. They're similar, but enough for a jury to decide beyond a reasonable doubt that they are the same person? Enough for a prosecutor to even bring the charges?"

"Right now, it's a stretch."

"What makes you think they are connected?"

"I spoke to someone in prison. He told me about his uncle who was doing all these terrible things. There's nothing on the books about it. He has an immaculate record, but it's a clue."

"But it's a clue to what?" I ask. "Did you follow him?"

"Yes, of course. That's all he's been doing," Mary Lou says.

"We were supposed to take a cruise to Alaska, but he doesn't have time for that."

"Mary Lou, please." He waves his hand in her direction. "This is important."

"Of course, because people's lives are at stake."

"Exactly," he says.

"Do you not believe that these cases are related?" I ask her. I have no doubt that Donald has told her plenty about this.

Her reaction makes me pause. Is Donald a crazy person, someone so obsessed with solving cases that he's looking for clues that aren't there?

"I'm not saying he's not on to something," Mary Lou says with a deep sigh. "I just wish that he could unplug from it once in a while. His retirement was supposed to be our time. We were no longer going to be tied to his work. Our vacations were not going to be focused on the cases that he was working on. I know that a trip like a cruise to Alaska may sound banal, but we have been married for almost fifty years and that should be worth something."

I can see the frustration, which she normally keeps buried deep, come bubbling to the surface. Trying to hide it, she goes to the kitchen to make another kettle of tea even though we're hardly through with this one.

"She's not wrong. It’s why I need your help. This has been consuming my life."

"Yes, I can see that," I say. "Tell me more about the cases."

"On the surface, they're not connected. The only thing connecting them was that they were assigned to me."

"To you."

He nods. "There were a number of cases that just never went anywhere. You know how many are actually solved? It's not like on television or in the movies. The vast majority of them are unsolved for years because you turn your attention to the ones that are more likely to have answers. They were assigned to me. I hadn't given them much thought. I mean, they were just cold cases. We all have cold cases. Then, I was interviewing a witness and I was going through my files when he mentioned that his uncle had been in these three locations where three of my victims were found. A runaway who was possibly trafficked, a little boy, and a 24-year-old woman, a graduate student. He was at those locations. This is a person I've never looked at before. He has no criminal record whatsoever. He works for a paper company."

“Which one?"

"Like Staples, but a small regional one called Boyden Paper."

"Tell me more about him," I say when he takes a long pause. He sits back down in the recliner and props his feet up.

"Sorry, I have a bad back," he says.

"Is that how you use the computer?"

He nods.

"He started a website and everything for himself," Mary Lou says, coming back with a fresh batch of snacks, this time with a few fruits and veggies, as well as more tea.

"I'm sorry about earlier," she adds. "I do believe in you, but like we talked, you need to understand where I'm coming from too."

“And I do.”

"I was going to save this for later, but since we made kind of a scene in front of our guest here--" He pulls out his phone and scrolls through something and then shows it to her. All I see is the name of a cruise line at the top.

"You got us tickets?"

"Yes. Two weeks from today. Pack your bags. We're off."

"Are you serious? A whole week in Alaska?"

"Just like you've always wanted," Donald smiles.

"That's amazing." She wraps her arms around her husband and kisses him on the lips. It has been years that they've been together, that much is clear. Yet it feels like they're newlyweds. They had a fight and made up in less than ten minutes in front of me. Nothing getting too serious or upsetting. I wonder if that's going to be us, Luke and me, years from now, only it's going to be me working around the clock to solve some impossible case and him complaining that we don't spend any time together.

He's not the workaholic that I am. Even now he is ready to retire because it doesn't make him happy. Personally, I've never really given that much thought. It's a good job, challenging enough to keep me on my toes. But happy? What is that? It's just the constant movement that I'm after, constantly being busy, searching for answers. Some of which are undoubtedly impossible to find, but that's what keeps me going. Something I've never admitted to many people out loud.

"You were telling me that this man who is the uncle of the guy from prison, he works for the Boyden Paper company?"

"Yes."

"They sell wholesale all around the region?"

"They do. They have a printing shop as well. I

visited it. It's north of Portland. He does a lot of sales, travels around."

"What makes you think that the cases are connected?"

"I'll tell you later," he says. "I just want to lay out the facts, names aside, okay?"

"Why, is he someone famous?"

"No, it's not a name you'll recognize at all. Just names come with biases, ethnicities, all sorts of garbage. But let me lay out the facts here. These are all cases I've had. They were all unsolved for a variety of reasons, mostly because there's absolutely no evidence in the majority of them."

"What makes you think that he had anything to do with this?"

"There were some other leads, we had interviewed them. They all have alibis. You know the drill. These cases are cold. Then, all of a sudden, this guy mentions not the people by name, but the locations of where the bodies were found, specific ones too. He mentions that his uncle did it. Don't you think that's a little fishy?"

Chapter 5

The longer I spent in this restored craftsman under the thick blanket of clouds in Olympia, Washington, the more brainwashed I seem to become. After talking to him for even a little bit, I'm suddenly on board, a conspiracy theorist as well. Everything he's saying is plausible, not just some kook making stuff up out of whole cloth. But as much as I want to deny it, the coincidences are not absurd. If you put this person's initials together, you make this number and this is the address of where so and so lives.

Therefore, the cases have to be connected. Trust me, I've seen plenty of those situations and I always have to force myself not to roll my eyes when I hear something like that. People who go for numerological conspiracies like that hold a special place in hell. But this is different.

"How would this guy in prison know the cases that you're handling?" I ask. "Did you ever bring them up?"

He shakes his head, no.

"How do you even know him? Why are you visiting him?"

"He was a witness in the murder of his own child. His wife killed her."

"Why is he in prison?"

"He committed major fraud, stole $2 million from Medicare. When the murder suicide happened, they started going through all of their financials and found it out."

"Are you sure that he didn't do it?" I ask, tilting my head to one side.

"Yes. He was on camera at the bar nearby. He had just gotten a restraining order from her, but don't think that I didn't consider it. How many family annihilators have done that exact same thing when their families were about to find out how much debt they were in and they were on the verge of being found out. In this case it was different. The mother had no idea. She had her own issues, actually, her own fraud, so the couple was a match made in hell, so to speak. He had no idea about the fraud she was committing with her retail store, and she had no idea about his, as far as anyone can tell."

"He was serving time."

“Where, in a white-collar prison?"

"Yes. Penitentiary. Five to ten years because he refused to take a plea. He thought that someone would take mercy on him because his daughter was killed, and of course it's a consideration, but he didn't seem sorry for any of the fraud that he committed. Don't worry about him, though. He’ll be out in three on good behavior."

"How did this come up? Why were you visiting him?"

"We talked about the Seahawks. We joked around a lot while the trial was happening. We're the same age. You could say that I made a friend, and I don't make friends often. Since he was in this predicament where no one would visit him, I decided to go out there."

"He actually went out there every other month. Can you believe it?"

"Look, I'm not like you, Mary Lou," Donald says. “I don’t meet people I like often. I know what you're going to say, all of your friends have husbands, but they like golf and I don't."

"Yes, I know. I used to think that being a golf widow would be terrible, but I'm a true crime widow, which is somehow even worse."

He looks at her, makes a face and they both laugh. At this point she's just joking. He had appeased her with a trip to Alaska, and that seems to be enough.

"You went to visit him and what, he told you right away?"

"No, it was probably the sixth visit. We had talked about all the terrible things that happened. We also talked about the Seahawks, anything and everything, the way that friends do."

"What happened then?" I ask. "How did he bring this up?"

"I just asked him if this were the most messed up thing that ever happened to him, that he'd ever heard of? He said, yes, but there was a close second. He said that he had a funny uncle and at first I thought that meant what people generally make it mean."

"And that is?"

"Well, a 'funny uncle' likes to molest kids, that kind of thing, but no. He said that one time he got drunk, like really drunk and that rarely happened. It was late at night. His father had died a long time ago and his uncle was just talking to him like he was his brother. They reminisced, they talked about why he'd been a bachelor for so long and why his marriage didn't work out. Then he all of a sudden said, 'You know, throughout all of that, I've always had a secret.'

When I asked him what secret, he said, 'I did some bad things, and a few people aren't living because of it.'"

"That's what he said, word for word?" I ask.

Donald nods.

“If this guy is your friend and you guys are the same age, his uncle is what?”

“He’s his uncle, but he’s the same age as him, seventy-five. He and his brother had a very big age gap, almost twenty years.”

“Got it,” I say. “So, what happened then?"

"This guy who I talked to in prison, I never told him about the cases I worked. I mentioned a few here and there. They had gone cold. We mostly talked about the ones that we had closed, prosecuted, that thing. Anyway, all of a sudden, he goes, ‘He told me where the bodies are,' and he named the locations."

"How exactly?"

"Cross streets. Then you walk down to the shore. When you walk through the forest, you get to this tree with this etching in it and you turn right. I wrote it all down, every detail. The guy told me that he had no idea what I was looking for. He had no idea what cases I had, but I had those locations memorized because I’d been there. I am the one who found all the evidence. You know that the location where you find the body it's like holy ground. It's a treasure trove of information."

I bite my lower lip, realizing that my mouth is now parched. I force myself to take a gulp of the tea, but it's no longer hot.

"You see, I may be a crazy conspiracy theorist, but I'm onto something, aren't I?"

"Yes, you definitely have something." I nod. "He knew the locations of these three victims?" I ask.

"Yes. He didn't know their names. Nothing else."

"What about who they were?"

"Some basic characteristics, but he said that he couldn't ask too many questions. He just let his uncle talk because he was scared of making him realize who he was talking to. He was drunk. He was just talking in the way that people do when they want to get something off their chest."

"What happened afterwards?" I ask.

"He never brought it up. He passed out, fell asleep, and my friend assumes that he had forgotten. He's half-scared, though, because he's getting out and his uncle's going to be the one to pick him up."

"That makes it a little dicey," I say.

He nods. "Yeah."

"What else?"

"I've done some research on him. No criminal record. Been married once. No instances, or at least no reported instances, of any sort of abuse. I haven't asked too many questions around the neighborhood, though. He had lived there for forty years. I'm assuming he has friends, neighbors, allies. I didn't want to draw too much attention. Not yet. Not until I have a plan."

"And you what, went to the FBI already and they said you were crazy?"

"Pretty much." He nods, hesitates for a moment, and then adds, "Actually, verbatim."

"So, they don't believe you?"

"No. They believe that I believe it. What about you, Kaitlyn?" he asks. "Do you believe me?"

Chapter 6

I had to leave his house for a little while, for a break. I said that I would be in touch, went to my rental car, sat under the cloud of rain, and watched the droplets collide with the windshield. It wasn't until I saw Mary Lou turn the light on in the living room and peek out from behind the curtains to check if were still there, that I started the engine, waved goodbye, and took off.

My thoughts were hard to process at first. I drove in circles around the old part of town, a few dilapidated buildings, tent enclosures, homeless teenagers walking around looking lost. When darkness descended, I got my phone out and texted Luke to tell him that everything was fine, but that I would be staying in a hotel in Olympia instead.

He asked if I could talk but I wrote, *Not yet. There's a lot here to go through.*

That part was true. Donald sounds like your tinfoil on the windows, visiting Roswell, New Mexico type of conspiracy theorist. I usually don't like to entertain those kinds of things, but something gives me pause. The story he told me is convoluted, complicated, and yet incredibly simple. This man suspects his uncle of killing three people. Three people who were in Donald's caseload, three people whose murderers were never found.

What are the chances of that?

But why come to me? Mostly because he's out of resources. He had tried so many other people. He tried his best to get them to talk, to move the cases forward, and there's no one else. That's why he brought up the information about my father, to leverage me into helping him.

What about my father? He told me some things that seem possibly accurate or true in some way, but it raised more questions than answers. My father was supposedly a witness to something big, and he has the files, but he's holding them hostage. I could try to break in sometime in the middle of the night. Of course, it's likely that a retired FBI agent is armed and ready with a response. What would be the point anyway? He's willing to give them to me if I cooperate and help.

Play private investigator. I have no jurisdiction here, after all.

I find the nearest Motel 6. It is the most basic of accommodations, no frills like shampoo. I'm shocked that there's soap, but it will do for a place to sleep. Plus, it's affordable. I imagine I will be staying in rooms like this for a very long time if I hope to save enough for a down payment on a condo, let alone a house in LA County. I unpack the minimal contents of my bag, sit down on the edge of the bed and stare at the small flat screen television, letting that blue color wash over me.

A sitcom plays in the background, the volume is muted. I hear people laughing, see the bright colors, and yet when I turn it up, I just get irritated. Their happiness, the complaints about their minor problems make me angry.

I call Luke, fill him in on what Donald and I had talked about. He's the only one who I can really talk to about any of this. I have few friends back home, and my family can't be bothered, not now.

My sister has just come back after the most traumatic experience of her life, and my mother, who was less than adequately prepared to even live her own life and mother us, is now dealing with her return. She is over the moon happy, of course, happy beyond words, but if I were to bring up the mystery around my father again, it would cause a rift. For a moment, we're back together as a family. We're happy, and I want to savor that happiness for as long as possible. But still, questions remain.

"You have to find out more," Luke says into the phone, his voice is coarse and serious. “He said that he knows something. Read the letter."

"He's the only one who might have any answers, but do I even want them?" I ask.

Not wanting to be separated, I turn on FaceTime on my iPad and place it in front of me on the slab of chipped Formica masquerading as a dining room table. Luke looks tired. The lighting is not doing him any favors, making his skin too white and draining all color from the tone. His mop of dark hair is falling slightly to the side, and I know that he has just come back from swimming.

We had started going to a local gym together. My sporadic workouts were not working out, and I wanted to get in better shape, at least keep my muscles from atrophying at the desk and behind the wheel. It's nice having that time together in the mornings. The gym has a pool, so Luke started doing long swims in addition to weightlifting. I hadn't looked at him from afar for a while, and here he was, his body chiseled and as sexy as ever. I wished more than anything that I were in his arms again rather than here in a soggy city under the pines confronting the possibility of discovering some dark secret about what may or may not have happened to my father.

"I know this is all weighing heavily on you," Luke says, pushing his hair out of his face.

He's off today, so he didn't bother with the shower.

"I just wish that you were here. I shouldn't have told you to stay behind. It's all just getting to be too much to handle."

"I know you didn't trust me with what happened in the desert. You went on your own and maybe that was the right thing to do because I would have tried to stop you. But in this case, I just want to be here for you. I have some experience. I mean, I do work for the FBI."

I nod, uncertain as to what to say. "I just don't know if I'm going to lose credibility with this guy if I suddenly bring my boyfriend in on this."

"Hey, maybe if you had a little less credibility, then he wouldn't be asking you to do all this investigating on your own."

"Yes, that's a good point. You think he'll just come right out and tell me what happened?"

"Maybe," he jokes, tilting back in his gamer chair.

He puts his leg up and I can see a little bit of his knee in the video.

"I miss you," I say. "I know I just left this

morning, but maybe it's like this teenage thing in me or something. I just want to be with you all the time."

"Look, you've been through a lot with your sister. Your caseload is just getting more intense."

"It's like I'm running on a treadmill," I say.

"What do you want? How can I help?" Luke asks.

He's always been good about that. Instead of telling me what to do or trying to find solutions, he listens carefully and then asks me what I want. I'm not so good in return. Whenever he has a problem, I scour my mind for what could possibly be wrong, find a million different solutions for how we can approach it, and try to solve it for him, when most of the time all you want to do is just have someone to vent to and that's about it.

"It's raining again," I say, walking over to the window and pulling up the darkening shades that smell like rubber and disinfectant. "This place is not the Marriott, that's for sure."

"I told you that you could stay in a nicer place. I have the points."

"Yes, I know." I shrug.

The rain is falling sideways now, and there are a few teenagers exchanging something in between handshakes as if every single rookie cop wouldn't know exactly what's going on. They're on bikes and there's a guy sitting in a car not too far away who delivers the drugs after the money is exchanged, thinking this will somehow protect them, but if there's any surveillance whatsoever, like from my vantage point or from the parking lot, the whole thing is recorded. While money is not directly exchanged for drugs, it's nevertheless made.

"Are you going to go talk to him again," Luke asks after I let the pause go too long.

I'm holding the iPad up now. It's in an awkward position next to my face and I wish I was on my phone instead. I sit back down facing the window and turn the overhead light on which casts horrendous shadows on my face.

"Sorry, I keep moving around," I say. "Sometimes it's easier to think when you're moving, you know? Can't exactly go on a walk right now."

"Why?"

"I'd get drenched," I say.

"Well, they do have these things called umbrellas," he jokes, giving me a smile.

I smile back and he points his finger at my face. "There you go. You can do it. Feeling better?"

"No, not really. Just keeping you entertained."

"We could do something else entertaining," he smiles, and when I look at him he gives me a wink.

"What are you talking about?" I gasp jokingly.

“Well, just you and me here, privacy of our own rooms and the internet.”

“Yes, and the internet.”

“But private video call and all.”

“What are you getting at, Mr. Galvinson?”

“You know what I’m getting at.”

He gives me a nod and tugs at his t-shirt.

“What if I were to just take this off?”

“Well, then you’d be shirtless,” I say, not taking the bait.

"Come on. Show me what you've got."

"No," I shake my head. "I can't."

"It'll take your mind off things."

"Maybe," I admit.

"It'll make you feel good."

"To what? Flash you?"

"And more."

I hesitate, looking at him. He pulls off his shirt, exposing his tan skin, wide shoulders, and a bit of the six pack that I know is just right there below the screen. I can't help it, I lick my lips.

"God, I wish you were here," I say.

"I am," he says. "Your turn."

Chapter 7

Anthony was looking forward to getting home that afternoon. It had been two weeks since he'd told Evelyn that he liked her and wanted to go out with her, a pivotal moment in his life up to that point. As a tenth grader, he had had crushes before in middle school but nothing ever materialized and he never felt comfortable enough to go ahead and ask a girl out. He didn't know what was going to happen afterwards, but by that Friday, he had given himself a deadline. He had waited long enough.

He knew that he liked her. It had been two months. If she were to turn him down, then that would be it. He would move on. Life was too short he had decided, to have secret crushes on them without them knowing. He had lost too many girls to "friends" territory as well and he had hoped that Evelyn wouldn't fall into that group.

Evelyn was a redhead. She had long, messy hair, mostly straight, but often wrinkled because she slept with it wet. She wore a little bit of makeup, and she had a sarcastic way of talking. Her parents were divorced, and she lived with her mom, just like he did, but in a big house in the fanciest neighborhood that was in their school district. Her dad had left her mom for a nurse at his hospital, but the alimony payments and the house made her quite comfortable, if not happy, Evelyn had told him.

Evelyn had joked about her mom's antidepressants but Anthony secretly sympathized because he was on them as well, especially in the wintertime when the cloud cover never abated. It was dark in the morning, and it was dark after school. The depression got bad sometimes. He had yet to tell Evelyn how sad he felt at times.

Anthony lived in a two-bedroom house in an old part of town. It was poverty old, not fancy old. It was working-class initially, and then just poor. It was the only place his mom could afford to live as a single hairdresser who worked in not a very nice salon, where people didn't leave tips. One of her biggest regrets in life was that she never went to college. As much as she liked hairdressing, she always told Anthony how important it was for him to go.

He had already picked out his reach schools and his safeties, and the ones that he would be glad to go to if they would have him. There was, of course, University of Washington and Washington State. There were other schools on the list, like California State University, Long Beach, and San Diego State because they were affordable and most importantly, they were in Southern California.

As a tenth grader, Anthony didn't know much of what he wanted to do with his life, except that he liked music. He would never be a concert pianist. He liked movies and he wanted to go somewhere warm and pretty by the ocean, like Southern California.

It had been exactly two weeks since he'd cornered Evelyn after last period by her locker and waited for everyone to clear out, making small talk. He then leaned over and said, "Hey, what are you doing tonight?"

She gave him a casual shrug without even looking up and said she was headed to the library, but she didn't really have any other plans. He waited for her to look up at him and see that this wasn't just him casually asking her about her weekend plans, this was more important than that. He was inviting her out on a date.

Anthony was scrawny, with a slim build for his age. He had shot up seven inches last summer and had somehow become even thinner. Evelyn, on the other hand, had a full bosom and wide hips and knew exactly what she had to offer besides a gorgeous body and a pretty face. Despite having some of the more popular boys in school being interested in her, something drew her to Anthony, and he'd felt it since they'd had their first art class together.

"I like you," he said, leaning on the locker, letting his hair fall in his face the way that guys did in his mom's romance novels.

You were supposed to be sultry and sexy, and you were supposed to say deep mysterious things that let the girl wonder about who you really were. He had realized that the problem with becoming too friendly with girls in the past was that the mystery had evaporated. They knew everything about him, and he knew everything about them, and there was just no way to transition to something more romantic after that.

With Evelyn, he would not make this mistake. It was no accident that he was wearing his very expensive leather jacket that he'd found in a thrift store in Seattle, which his mom had let him buy despite the fact that it was $95. It was a great find but not one that he could really afford, and so it cost him three of his weekly allowances and he knew that it was a splurge for his mom as well.

"I like you," Anthony repeated, looking straight into Evelyn's eyes. He held the gaze so long, it made him feel uncomfortable but again, from his mom's novels, he knew this was absolutely necessary in order to catch her off guard.

Evelyn had tilted her head and looked up at him with a furrowed brow. Something had changed between them, something they wouldn't be able to get back to, but he held on strong. This was the bravest thing he had ever done. Tell a girl how he felt, and remain standing there, disarmed, waiting for her reply. A smile floated over her face, brightening her eyes.

"I like you too," she said quietly.

Then without asking permission but knowing that he had it, he leaned over, tilted her chin up a little bit, and pressed his lips to hers. This was his first kiss, and when she opened her mouth and their tongues touched, he knew that his life would never be the same again.

For two weeks, Anthony and Evelyn were inseparable. They saw each other at school as much as they could, made plans every day Evelyn's mom would allow, which wasn't nearly often enough, and talked on the phone and texted each other late into the night.

They did homework together with their

computers open and the video chats on, listening to the same music, and just enjoying being in each other's company.

Today, she was coming over right after school. In fact, she was waiting outside while he cleaned up a little bit. His mom worked long hours late into the night, and so it was his responsibility to clean and do chores.

They weren't certain whether Evelyn's mom would let her come over after school today, so he didn't bother to do it early in the morning. Now he was embarrassed by the plates piling up in the sink, dirty dishes all over the coffee table, and mostly his room, and the unmade bed piled with books and papers everywhere. He was so embarrassed, he made Evelyn wait outside but after ten minutes, it got too cold, and she let herself in.

"Look, I don't care how dirty it is, let me just wait in here, okay?"

Despite all the time they spent together, and all the minutes they had kissed and made out, he was still a little bit uncertain about her coming over to his house. She lived in an almost 3000-square foot home out in the fancy suburbs, with a two-car garage and a basement, an enormous staircase that was straight out of the movies. His house was a cramped two-story with small rooms, a tiny porch, and four cats that he loved, but the smell of their litter boxes, not so much.

Nevertheless, Evelyn seemed to find everything about his home fascinating. She didn't even mind the half-painted wall where multiple coats of ivory were needed to cover the bright orange, a project that his mother had started three weeks ago and then never had a chance to get back to.

When the house was ready, Anthony and Evelyn sat down on the couch, turned on the TV, and devoured a bag of pretzels. He had offered to order pizza, but Evelyn declined knowing that he wouldn't let her pay and that it was going to be too expensive for him.

What she hadn't told Anthony yet was that she actually loved him. She knew right from their first kiss. For two weeks she had waited for him to say it to her, but he hadn't. A mild disappointment. When she knew that, she just had to keep waiting for--

"You want to watch *Stranger Things* again from the beginning?" Anthony asked.

As they scrolled through Netflix, trying to find a new show to binge, that's when she knew that she just couldn't wait any longer.

"I love you," Evelyn said.

He turned to face her. "I'm supposed to say it first."

"Well, you didn't."

She reached over and kissed him on the mouth.

"I love you too," Anthony said.

"You're not saying that just to be nice, right?" she asked, tilting her head in that curious way that always made him melt.

"No, not at all."

"Good. Because I really, *really* love you," she said.

"I really, really love you too," he said and pushed her back against the couch. He kissed her again and again and they fell into the pillows.

They spent the rest of the afternoon on cloud nine, almost in another plane of existence.

Everything was good because they were together.

Nothing could ever be wrong.

What neither of them knew was that this would be the last normal day in their life, and their happiness would soon burst like a balloon that had gotten too full of hot air.

Chapter 8

Cora was tired. It had been a long day at the salon and her feet ached, despite wearing a pair of $200 sneakers that her son, Anthony, had insisted that she purchase in order to cushion her body against the wear and tear of being on her feet for hours. Her work hours were erratic, but she tried to take at least one day a week off. She was working on taking two in order to spend time with her son, who was growing up way too fast. She wanted to go on hikes and get some of that much needed exercise in order to function with her multiple sclerosis diagnosis.

Her body was breaking down. Her work wasn't doing her any favors, but she loved the salon. She loved her clients, and she couldn't imagine doing anything else. She knew there would be a time when she probably wouldn't be able to work on her feet much longer and she was preparing for that by taking classes at South Puget Sound Community College toward an eventual bachelor's degree in counseling.

Besides hair, her favorite thing was psychology. She wanted to work with children, especially elementary school kids, and help them deal with the turbulent lives that their sometimes-well-meaning parents had created for them.

Cora knew a little bit about relationship trauma herself. The terrible marriage to her first husband had convinced her never to marry again, despite the fact that she was not yet even forty. Trim, with a nice figure and a friendly personality, she was a catch by all accounts, but the pain from her first divorce made her promise to herself to never rely on a man again.

As she cleaned up her station to get it ready for tomorrow, she made small talk with Sarah, the oldest stylist who worked at the salon. She was well into her sixties but looked like she could be 45, having spent most of her excess cash on various medical procedures and nips and tucks, as well as an expensive eye cream and everything else that she could afford to help keep aging at bay.

Sarah was an inspiration to Cora in many ways. She had never worked until she turned fifty, because that's when her husband decided to leave her for a younger woman. She had refused to take even a penny of alimony or child support despite having three kids to raise. They were sharing custody, of course, but nothing else. She wanted none of his money, even though she was left almost penniless and unable to pay the rent.

Cora knew this was probably foolish, but she admired the older woman's pride and confidence in her ability to make it on her own. Sarah always said she was proud of the fact that she'd gotten as far as she had in life. In fact, when she opened the salon, she sent her ex-husband a thank you note and a basket of fruit, showing gratitude because him leaving allowed her to discover who she really was and what she was really capable of as a person.

Cora was looking forward to getting home, it had been a long day and her MS was flaring up, making her feel more tired than usual by the end. While Windexing the mirror, she saw that her roots had grown in from the color she'd applied three weeks ago, and she wondered which way she should go next. Unlike many hairdressers who let their hair go or indulged in off the wall looks, Cora took pride in maintaining the kind of hair that her clients came to her to achieve.

It was hard to color your own hair, but she had gotten used to it over the years, even perfecting hard techniques like balayage.

Her son Anthony had seen her color her hair

since he was a kid and was always quite interested in the process, but it wasn't until he hit ninth grade that she actually let him wear his hair dyed at school.

Usually bright colors like pink and green were reserved exclusively for the summer months, especially when he was in middle school. The school didn't have any particular rules about it, but she didn't want the teachers to judge her son too harshly, like she remembered the way her own teachers talked about her when she was in school.

Anthony attended a public school in a very good school district, and they already had a lot of things stacked up against them. She was a single mom when everyone else in the Honors and AP courses were married couples. She couldn't participate in the parent-teacher association because her hours were erratic, and they always held it on the first Tuesday of every month at 9:00 AM sharp.

She tried to volunteer and to participate with the other moms, but it was hard to make friends. Some were suspicious about her as a single woman, rarely inviting her to events and dinner parties in their homes because everyone else was coupled. Even though dating had not been a priority for her for a very long time, her son had gotten old enough to realize that something was wrong about his pretty, young mom being completely on her own. Unlike other kids who would have hated a stepfather because they had been in and out of their lives, Anthony just had his mom, her parents, and his father and his new family across town.

A few months ago, Anthony even asked his mom, "How come you don't date anyone anymore? You know that you can tell me if you're into girls, right? I'll still love you."

He was being his usual sarcastic, smartass self, and she liked that best about him. He kept her on her toes, not disrespectful in any way, just sweet and kind, her little boy forever.

"You know why," Cora said, turning the conversation back to his father, but this time Anthony didn't buy it.

"Come on, it can't just be all about him. He didn't want to be with you, so what?"

"It has nothing to do with that." Cora said. "I'm way over him, and I know that he's perfectly happy with Melinda and I'm happy for them. Regardless of how he treated me, he deserves happiness."

She said this and for the first time in a long time she actually meant it. Her relationship with her ex-husband had improved considerably, even though it was never that toxic on her end, she wanted what was best for Anthony, and she wasn't going to use him as a pawn in a convoluted custody battle. The fact that she didn't take any money from her ex helped the matter tremendously, but it also made Melinda suspicious of her for many years. It wasn't until they got to know each other that they actually became somewhat friendly.

However, what Anthony did not know was that for the last two months Cora had been seeing someone. Steven Hildebrand was the owner of an auto mechanic shop, he had never been married, he didn't have any kids, and he was desperately in love with her. She knew this as sure as she knew that the sky was blue. He had been saying as much for a few years now, even if he never actually said the words.

Cora and Steven had met each other years ago at the mall when he was dating a friend of hers. They broke up and Cora had made a promise to herself to never date any of her friends' boyfriends, so he was permanently put into an untouchable file. Or at least that is what she told herself at the time.

The relationship between Steven and her friend was not particularly long or deep, no more than a few months. In fact it was Cora's friend who had broken up with Steven, but none of that mattered.

Cora liked having Steven in the friend group, and Steven hung around and wanted to be around her in whatever capacity that he could. He dated other women on and off, but none of them stuck because his heart really belonged to the sarcastic, witty, no-nonsense hairdresser at Hair Bliss studio.

When she turned him down for dates a few times, he started making appointments to get his hair cut and colored just to spend more time with her. She knew this, of course, especially when the appointments were the last ones of the day so that they could spend more time talking and getting to know each other.

Their relationship would've continued this way for a while, probably years longer, if Steven Hildebrand had not received an offer to buy his business from a chain auto shop valuing it at way more than he ever dreamed it could be sold for. Suddenly the possibility of retiring at such an early age and moving somewhere sunny, Arizona, Nevada, California, became a real option. He had turned to his friend Cora to ask her advice and it wasn't until she was faced with the reality of him leaving and not being around much longer that she realized just how she'd felt about him all of these years.

The next time he came in to get his hair cut they were alone in the studio after everyone else had left. He put on some of her favorite music from the 90s on the speakers and asked her to dance, the way he often did, even though she mostly said no.

This time, however, she didn't. They danced their hearts out. When he leaned in to kiss her, she kissed him back. For two months, Cora and Steven had been inseparable. They saw each other often after work. Sometimes for lunch breaks and on runs.

Anthony was busy with school and his own social life, so he didn't pay much attention. Cora liked it that way because she wasn't ready to tell him that there may be somebody important for him to meet. She didn't worry that he wouldn't approve. She knew that he probably would, because Steven was reliable, easygoing, confident, and fun. He was a low-pressure kind of guy. She knew that Anthony would like that about him, but still she was nervous.

What if something went wrong? What if her son didn't like the one man that she loved and she would be forced to choose?

Today was the day.

Anthony didn't know it yet, but Steven was going to pick her up from work. They were going to drive together back to her house, and she was going to introduce him as her boyfriend.

Cora had thought on and off about how to do this for a week now. Maybe invite him to Sunday dinner, maybe for casual Saturday brunch, but she'd decided that in the evening after school over a couple of slices of pizza would be the best way to go. If Anthony's girlfriend, Evelyn, was there, it might even help matters. Cora liked her very much. It was a brand new relationship, but she had a good influence on Anthony. She had her priorities in order, had college on the horizon and planned to make something of her life.

Cora took one long look around the studio. She had not only cleaned her station but also swept the floor, organized the magazines, and picked up a few things here and there, before the official cleaners came later.

She was always like that, trying to do her part, to help people the most that she could. Sometimes people took advantage, and she made a note of that, but most of the time she received her good deeds back threefold.

Cora glanced at her phone, no messages from Steven. He would be here in a few minutes. She put on her coat, grabbed her purse and sat down on one of the chairs out front, in front of the reception desk to wait.

What she did not know was that this would be the last time she would ever clean up after a long day at work.

Chapter 9

After making out on the couch well into the first episode of *Stranger Things*, Anthony and Evelyn suddenly separated. It wasn't one of them pulling away, it was both just stopping when Anthony's hands started to slide under her shirt and it went a little bit too far. Pressing their bodies against one another was one thing, this was something else that they hadn't talked about. They didn't trust their bodies quite yet.

Anthony shifted onto the far cushion and Evelyn sat up adjusting her shirt. She looked at the time, it was 6:30, and he wondered when his mom was finally coming back. He saw Evelyn looking at her phone, tilted his head to one side, letting his hair fall on his face.

"Wow, she's like half an hour late, right?"

"She was supposed to be here at six? Or was she going to leave then?"

"She was going to get off at 5:40 or so. She said she wanted to have dinner with us." Anthony said, "Steven is coming over for dinner too."

"Who's Steven?" Evelyn asked.

"They've been friends for a while. He gets haircuts there and I guess they like to go running together."

"Do you think they're doing anything else?" Evelyn asked.

"Oh, please." Anthony rolled his eyes and stuck out his tongue, grossed out.

"You know your mom is hot, right?" Evelyn said. "And she's all alone. It's not right."

"So, if she wasn't hot, then it would be okay?"

"No, I'm not saying that," Evelyn shrugged. "I'm just saying that she's still sort of young. I mean, she's, what, forty? Plus, she looks like she's thirty. Any guy would be happy to be with someone like that."

"Well, she's not interested."

"Are you sure? What about this Steven guy? Does he usually come over for dinner?"

"He used to, and then I didn't see him for a while. I guess they made plans again," Anthony said, totally oblivious. But Evelyn was on to something. She could feel it.

Anthony looked at the time again. While

walking around the house, he cleaned up the mess that they'd made from snacking. He threw away the paper towels that they had used like napkins.

He was starting to feel antsy. This wasn't like his mom. He picked up his phone, checked that there were no messages or calls that he had missed, and then texted, *Where are you?*

He had the read receipts on, but when he checked his phone again, it didn't say that the message was read. He knew that his mom's phone was practically surgically attached to her hand.

With every passing minute, the anxiety in the pit of his stomach got worse and worse. "What's wrong?" Evelyn asked. "She'll be here soon, I'm sure."

"No, you don't know her. If she were going to be late, she would text me. It's been almost an hour now and nothing. She's not even replying to any of the text messages."

"Look, maybe she's busy. Maybe she has a client."

"But she didn't have a client, and if she got one, she would tell me about it," he said.

"Then I wouldn't worry. You know, the two of you are a little bit too connected."

Anthony glared at Evelyn. She had no right to talk to him that way. This was his mom, and yes, he worried about her. He wasn't sure what to do, so he dialed the number of the studio and let the phone ring until it reached voicemail. Then he called two of her coworkers, both of whom said that they had left earlier around 5:00, as this was one of the Fridays that they'd all decided to close up shop early and get some much-needed rest and relaxation with their families.

Before hanging up with Jeffrey, the 25-year-old apprentice, whom his mom had taken under her wing, Anthony asked him to please be honest.

"Can you just tell me if my mom had no plans after work, or what could have happened? I mean, this is really not like her. You know how close we are."

"No, I don't know of any plans," Jeffery said. "She was just going to stay late or clean up a little bit, get her stuff in order and go home. She said she was looking forward to having dinner with you. She was going to tell you about Steven."

The words just came out just like that.

"What do you mean tell me about Steven?"

"Oh, crap," Jeffrey said.

Even though Anthony couldn't see it, he knew that he had put his hand over his mouth. Jeffrey wasn't good at keeping secrets. He could probably make a stereotypical joke about him being a hairdresser, but everyone else at the salon was much better. If you told them something in private, they kept it to themselves, not even sharing it among their co-workers. That's one of the reasons why the customers stayed so loyal. They knew that no one talked about them behind their backs.

Sometimes, even good news wouldn't travel that well and customers would have to tell each of the hairdressers individually in order for them to hear. That's the way that Cora liked it. She wanted everyone to feel comfortable coming to her and put everyone at ease. She wasn't going to run some 'cool girl clique' as she called it because she had worked at too many salons that had that exact approach.

"I'm sorry, I can't tell you. She's going to kill me," Jeffrey said.

"Please. You know this is serious. You know that she would never not get in touch with me," Anthony said. "I mean, we had plans to have dinner together with Evelyn and Steven. He was going to come over. What was the big news about him? It may have something to do with this."

Jeffrey was new to the salon, new to hairdressing, but he was also very familiar with Cora and her strict rules about gossip. "I really can't say. I've already said too much," Jeffrey said and hung up the phone.

For the first time in his life, Anthony had the urge to slam down his phone, if only it had a receiver, like they did in *Stranger Things*.

If he were to slam his phone down, he'd lose all access to communication and his mom would not be very happy having to buy him another one anytime soon. Instead, he threw it on the couch and gritted his teeth. "I guess she had plans with Steven, but he was going to come over anyway."

"Do you know his number?" Evelyn asked. Anthony sat down on the couch. He nervously tapped his foot on the ground pressing his fingers into the thickness of his palm over and over again. It was a nervous tic that he'd developed when he was a sixth grader to cope with bullying by the popular kids at school. He had bitten his fingernails as well. Both things he'd managed to stop doing largely with help from his mom but now, without her here, all of these little coping strategies returned with a vengeance.

He picked up his phone and searched for Steven's number, but he couldn't find it. "What was his last name again?"

Wiener. Steven Wiener? He said to himself. No, that didn't sound right.

"Steven Pacella? Andrews? Gilbert?" Some of these were writers and others were people from school.

"Steven King," Evelyn suggested and cracked a smile. Any other time Anthony would have laughed. In this case, the joke didn't land.

Instead, he just buried his head in his hands. He prayed to God that he was exaggerating, that he was freaking out for no reason. He prayed to a

God that he wasn't even sure that he believed in that he was worried over nothing, that this was just some misunderstanding.

His mom was human after all. Maybe she forgot. Maybe she got a flat tire. No, that couldn't be right. He looked outside. Her car was parked out there. She must have gotten a ride from a friend. Not something unheard of. Ever since the gas prices had gone up his mom had tried to find ways to save money.

The studio was also not very far away from their house, directly along the bus line. Maybe she had taken the bus there. Anthony had no way of finding out whether she had or hadn't done any of these things.

Finally, when an hour and a half had passed, he dialed 911. He didn't confirm or announce this to Evelyn in any way, but her eyes got big like saucers when she heard him say, "Hello, officer. I don't know if this is the right number to call, but my mom is missing. She was supposed to come home an hour and a half ago from work. She didn't. She just disappeared."

"An hour and a half? Is this an emergency?" The operator asked.

"Yes, of course. No, what I mean is there's something wrong."

"Do you know that something has happened to her? Does she need an ambulance?"

"No, she's just not here. I called her work. She's supposed to be here, and she was going to text me no matter what."

Anthony was speaking quickly jumping all around. Drowning in his words. The operator managed to calm him down just enough for him to grab a piece of paper and write down a non-emergency number for somebody else at the precinct. As soon as the line disconnected, he was angrier than ever.

"They said that this isn't an emergency. I mean, if this isn't an emergency, then what is?"

"Anthony, you have to take a few deep breaths, okay? Chances are she's completely fine. What 911 probably said is that she's not hurt. She's not bleeding. She doesn't need the ambulance and the fire truck and all of them to come right this minute."

"Yes, exactly. Because we have no idea where she is. Why won't anyone believe me that this is a big deal?"

"I believe you. I know that it is, but we should take some measured steps. Right? We have to figure out what could have happened, maybe go to the studio, maybe go to the hair salon."

"But how?" He said shaking his head. He hadn't gotten his driver's license yet, and Evelyn was going to get picked up by her mom later this evening.

"Okay, look, let's call this number. There's going to be a cop on the other end. He's going to tell us what to do. Okay? It's going to be fine."

Anthony nodded, hoping more than anything in the world that she was right. Knowing that, in fact, something terrible must have happened.

His mother would never not get back to him. His mother would never not return his calls.

What if it was an accident? What if she lost her phone, dropped it in the toilet, or stepped on it and it broke? What if she couldn't call him? Why wouldn't she answer if she were still at the studio? The questions kept coming like an avalanche.

Evelyn managed to get him to dial the non-emergency number and wait for someone to reply.

The hours that came after passed like molasses, every minute was accounted for and cataloged. There was nothing Anthony could do to help the situation one bit. Nothing would distract him from the fact that his mom was gone, nothing could convince him that she was okay. The more time that passed, the more he realized that he had been right all along. That was what was the worst thing. Evelyn had called her mom and asked for a little bit more time. Finally, her mom had agreed, but wouldn't give her any more time past ten pm.

When Mrs. Ware arrived, she was expecting to

see two teenagers huddled up on the couch pretending like they hadn't been fooling around all night. What she did not expect to see was two frightened kids sitting at opposite ends of the couch staring into space, lost and confused, and mostly sad. Evelyn and her mom did not have a close relationship the way that Anthony and Cora did. Her mom didn't understand her.

Mrs. Ware had friends who were going through divorce, chemotherapy treatments and parents with Alzheimer's. She was so engrossed in this adult world that she had forgotten that her teenager needed someone to relate to her too. But Mrs. Ware didn't understand TikTok, didn't like contemporary music and had very little interest in nostalgia shows on Netflix, because, according to her, they didn't portray what life was really like in the 80s. So if anything, the gulf between her and her daughter kept getting bigger and bigger.

She was secretly hoping for her daughter to turn twenty or twenty-five so that she would again have something to talk to her about, mainly herself. Walking over Anthony's threshold, the last thing that she was expecting was for her daughter to run into her arms and give her a warm hug.

"Thanks for coming," Evelyn said practically on the verge of tears.

"What happened?" Mrs. Ware asked immediately suspicious. Had this boy done something to her daughter that she didn't want?

But given the fact that Anthony hadn't even bothered to look up she knew that there was something else going on. It took Evelyn a few sentences to catch her up, and in that moment, Mrs. Ware realized that it was up to her to somehow solve this problem. She asked questions and Anthony replied looking somewhere straight ahead in a state of shock.

"So, you called the police?"

"Yes, the 911 number and they said it wasn't an emergency and then the non-emergency number. The guy told me that I had to wait much longer to actually make a missing person's report, but the problem is that she's missing right now, and by tomorrow morning if something has happened to her or someone has taken her, she's going to be so much further away. How are they ever going to find her? They're wasting time."

Unlike before Anthony was now talking with a sense of dread and calm that was difficult for Mrs. Ware to process, there was a detachment in his voice like he was there, but he was somewhere else. She sat down next to him and took his hands in hers to try to snap him out of it.

"Listen, I'm going to help you the best I can."

"What are you going to do?" he asked.

"Your father, did you call him?"

He looked away.

"They're not close," Evelyn said.

"Yes, but you still have to call him. What if he knows something that you don't? If she was in a car accident?"

"Of course," Anthony said, "the hospitals, I didn't call any of the hospitals."

"First we have to call your father." Mrs. Ware took control of the situation. Though Anthony wanted to make the call himself, she did it for him.

Mr. Rydell answered on the second ring "Anthony, what's wrong?" Clearly not expecting a call so late from his son on a day that they were not expected to be in touch. Mrs. Ware introduced herself and updated him on the situation.

"I was just wondering if there was a chance that you had heard from Anthony's mother, maybe she called you or someone had called you?"

"No, not at all. Yes, that is so strange. She's usually very punctual. That is one of the things that she hated most about me."

Mrs. Ware rolled her eyes wondering if her ex-husband would make a remark like that about her fifteen years later.

She talked in a hushed tone taking the phone to the kitchen and telling Anthony and Evelyn to stay back. At first Anthony was going to protest, but then he just gave up. It was good to have someone take over and try to handle the situation. When Mrs. Ware hung up, however, he did not like the result.

"Your father's going to come and take you home."

"No, I'm staying right here."

"Anthony, you're under eighteen. You're not going to stay at home by yourself overnight."

"I'll be fine."

"Have you ever stayed by yourself before?"

"No, but I've been on a camping trip."

"That's not the same," Mrs. Ware shook her head. "I'm going to wait here until your father comes and then maybe he'll help you look for your mom."

"No, he won't. He'll just drive me twenty miles over to his house, and I won't be here to answer any calls in case she does call for help in any way. Thanks for nothing."

He started to sob, tears streaming down his face. For a moment Mrs. Ware wondered if she had made a mistake, maybe she should have taken him to look for his mom, but where? She wasn't sure, and if the police weren't making a big deal out of this, then it had to be fine, right? Maybe she just went with a boyfriend, forgot, lost track of time or maybe she was in a car accident. Either way, he couldn't stay here by himself. Calling his father was the right thing to do. Still, she looked to her daughter for approval. Evelyn gave her a shrug. She didn't know how to handle this any more than her boyfriend. They waited for a while.

Mrs. Ware was expecting the father to jump into his car and drive over right away, but it was a good two hours before he bothered to show up.

"How far away does he live again?" Mrs. Ware asked.

"Twenty-five minutes."

"Sorry, I got into this whole thing with my wife," Mr. Rydell said when he arrived.

"You mean that she doesn't want me to come over?" Anthony snapped.

"It has nothing to do with that."

"What else could it be about?"

For a moment, Mrs. Ware had a tinge of regret. Perhaps she hadn't handled this right.

"Anthony would like to go by the salon."

"It's twenty minutes the other way. No."

"Dad, we have to. I'm not going to go with you if we don't."

"Did you call?" he asked.

"Yes. But what if she can't answer the phone? What if she's hurt? I want to stop by the salon and at least see that she's okay."

"Fine," Mr. Rydell said giving in. "What's another hour or so? Not exactly looking forward to going back home to continue round two of that fight," he said to Mrs. Ware as if she were a long-time friend.

She felt nothing but annoyed. She didn't know Cora well, but the few times that they had spoken she knew that this man was the complete opposite of her. She found him irritating and annoying and was glad that he was no longer part of Cora's life.

Mrs. Ware put her arm around her daughter expecting her to shrug her off, but she didn't. Instead, she tucked in tighter, giving her a warm hug, the kind that she hadn't felt in almost a year. When she glanced over at Anthony, she saw that there was nothing but distance between him and his father, a distance that would grow even bigger in the days to come.

Chapter 10

I sleep in late tossing and turning all night. I rarely have dreams, but on this occasion, I have one where my teeth fall out and crumble into my hands, but I only remember this when I grab my phone in the morning and see what I had looked up on Google the night before. What does a dream about missing teeth mean? Apparently, it means you're feeling anxious and out of control. Big surprise there. I don't like getting cases in this manner.

I like to get them assigned from the Lieutenant, get some brief details involving the victim or missing person, then conducting a series of interviews to get to the bottom of what might have happened, as well as processing the forensic evidence. I don't like to be blackmailed into working on other cases that I have nothing to do with, forced to do private investigative work in order to get some clues to the mystery surrounding my father.

In the morning, when I take a shower, I'm angry more than anything else. Who does Donald think he is, calling me up here, filling my head with all of these lies and secrets, and how can I trust him anyway?

If he would go out of his way like this, to lie to me about the most basic things, how can I believe he will tell me the truth about something this big? Anyone else in his position would just come forward and tell me what it is that he has on my father and help me figure it out. Then maybe, just maybe I'd work with him on his cold cases, but the truth is that cold cases are nearly impossible to solve.

It's not like in the movies. You don't just need to be an investigator who can put pieces together that others can't. There's more to it. You've got to get people to talk who haven't talked before, and probably have no interest in revealing any secrets to any strangers whatsoever.

It's one of the reasons why cold cases stay cold and the mystery remains for a lifetime, because the people who aren't willing to talk, aren't going to talk. They have way too much to lose.

I come out of the shower, wrap myself in the towel, and sit on the edge of the bed for a few moments, trying to make a decision as to where to go from here. If I go back to Donald and Mary Lou's, I'm saying yes, helping him solve his cases in an effort to get the answers I want. Frankly, I have no idea why he even needs my help. He has someone willing to talk to him from prison about his uncle, he's got some sort of lead, so why does he need me?

There are still so many unknowns, but I won't get any of these answers unless I agree to work with him, but do I want to enter this relationship at all?

Do I want to bother with getting involved? For what? To open up old wounds that probably won't mean much anyway?

This all goes back to exactly how much I believe his story about my father. On one hand, he has no reason to lie, on the other hand, he has every reason to obfuscate the truth. If he wants my help, if he wants one law enforcement officer to believe in him and help him, then I'm as good as any when everyone else has given up.

There's a knock on my door.

"I'm still here, please come back later," I say expecting it to be housekeeping, but the knock persists. I guess she didn't hear me, I decide, walking out and opening the door. My mouth drops open when I see him.

Luke's arrival here is a surprise, but a nice one. He had booked the flight as soon as we got off the phone, and taken an overnight to Seattle and driven down. He didn't look nearly as tired as I did, after having a full night's sleep.

"I can't believe you're here," I say pulling him close to me, and inhaling the sweet scent of his body. Not so much an odor, but the scent of sand and coconut shampoo and home that I had no idea that I'd missed so much.

"It sounded like you missed me," Luke said.

I wanted to ask him so much more, like why he came now, he really didn't need to, and a million other things.

But instead of talking, he just pulls me close to him and kisses me. He presses his body against mine, and our hands start to move on their own, pulling off each other's clothes. He pulls me on top of him, and onto the bed, burying his hands in my hair. His hands are everywhere all at once, and our bodies become one. Afterwards, with the sheets all crinkled, and our bodies wrapped up in each other's, we fall into a deep sound sleep without a single worry on our minds.

Our decision to go on a hike is spontaneous. Just one of those out-of-the-blue ideas that strikes your fancy in the morning and you just go with it. I do a quick search on Google for hiking near Olympia, Washington.

For some reason I was expecting it to be difficult to find a trail, but once I started looking, I saw that there were more than a few wonderful contenders. There are short busy trails near DuPont with old gravel roads leading up to the parking lot, running along the abandoned railroad tracks, and toward the beach it's a short, scenic, and flat route, but Luke shakes his head no, he wants something a little bit more private. There's the Nisqually National Wildlife Refuge with trail lengths of one to ten miles, about twenty minutes from Olympia.

"It has a river estuary with a lot of wildlife and a system of boardwalks and viewing points. The hike can be as long or short as you like, but the birding is the largest attraction," I read off the website. "There are plenty of benches and picnic areas for taking breaks and trail maps are around."

"That sounds nice, but let's go somewhere away from people, somewhere we can be alone." He gives me a wink. I can't help but smile back. The Mima Falls west trail looks gorgeous in the photos. It seems like a gentle walk through the woods and is listed as a popular area with many trails sprawling all around through the Capital State Forest. I continue the search for the perfect spot. I want to see some waterfalls and definitely put Tumwater Falls on my list as a necessary place to visit before we leave. Apparently, it's got a lot of old buildings like mills, hydroelectric installations, colonial buildings, and even the old Olympia brewery.

"What about Lost Valley or the Sherman Creek Loop?" I say showing him a few pictures. "The trail length is over eight miles with an elevation gain of over 1200 feet. I mean, we can really challenge ourselves, but I think I have to get back in touch with Donald."

"Sure, let's go there," he suggests.

We grab a little bit of water and I change into yoga pants and a t-shirt with a long sleeve jacket and head for the trails and the capital forest through some classic Pacific Northwest wilderness. When we get there, I realize that this is the perfect place for us.

Three miles in, and we hardly see more than a few people. The remote location makes it quiet and tranquil, but the trails are also clearly marked making me feel better about not getting lost. As we make our way through the wooded valley and along a quietly flowing creek, I lose myself in the greenness that surrounds me.

At the beginning of the trail, there is a creek that continues for quarter of a mile before splitting off. We follow along the small ridge to where Sherman and Lost Valley Creeks meet and around the bend, the trail splits again, both sides, keeping us on the Lost Creek Trail.

The lushness of the Pacific Northwest never ceases to amaze me. As much as I love the mountains of Southern California, and the deserts and wildness that comes with them, it's different here.

There's privacy to it. The creek tumbles by, the pine trees close in and everything is dripping in wetness. As I walk on the trail, the twigs don't even snap under my feet because they're so waterlogged. The sun, somewhere above the clouds, filters its way through the dew hanging on the branches.

I remember that somewhere, in another life, there's a place where the sun shines almost all the time. We hike our way along the creek and I pick up a few pebbles here and there, putting a few in my pocket for good luck. It's something I've done for a while, collecting little pieces of nature from wherever we go. I know that it's probably not right, but it makes me feel good to have these collections of rocks and these bottles of sand from the various beaches that I have frequented.

We talk about nothing at all. One of those conversations that means so much more than its content. Over the last few months, Luke and I have gotten so close, it's almost hard to be apart. Some might call our relationship toxic or incredibly codependent and perhaps it is, but it also feels good.

I love spending time with him, and I want to be with him all the time. He makes me laugh and I make him smile. We seem to just get each other in that way that you go through life just hoping to find someone who would. We don't have too much in common in terms of things we like to watch or read, but I'm interested in hearing him talk about what he likes to watch and read. He's interested in hearing me talk about what I like to watch and read.

Our conversations become a never-ending cycle of relaying things we've learned or seen. Though it's probably nothing that I would have read myself, I find it fascinating when he tells me about it.

"It's almost hard to breathe here, isn't it?" Luke says.

"What do you mean?"

"I don't know. Just the air is so heavy with moisture. I feel like I take a breath and it's like all inside of me."

The humidity is wearing on me. Feels like there's this point where it will just get to be too much, and it'll be too cold and then a little bit too warm. Somewhere in the distance, I hear the chirping of the birds and the bubbling of the creek and then I realize that I have to go to the bathroom. I check the map. The nearest one is miles away, but the urgency gets worse with every minute.

"I'm going to go ahead a little bit and duck behind a tree or something, okay? You stay behind."

He nods giving me a smile.

"Watch out. Let me know if anyone's coming."

I don't think anyone's going to be here anywhere near this place. Well, anyway, I don't want to gross anybody out by peeing out here. I've never had a problem going to the bathroom outside. In fact, I actually prefer it over the stinky public national park bathrooms and campground bathrooms that are rarely cleaned and almost never have any toilet paper.

I have nothing against the parks themselves. It's just that, for some reason, the campground bathrooms tend to be a bit neglected.

I walk a little bit ahead, looking out to the creek, and hide myself behind a pine tree. I venture into the forest as much as I can without totally drenching my legs and with the cool air coming off the creek, I know that I'm not going to dry anytime soon if I do get wet.

I pull down my pants, relieve myself, and then just as I pull them back up, something touches me. It's probably just a leaf, so I push it away without paying much attention, but it comes back and hits my leg. When I roll my leggings back up, I lean over, look around the bush and scream at the top of my lungs.

She's attached to the tree, with her shoulders tied tightly to the trunk. Her arms are laced over the branches and tied as well.

Her mouth is slightly open, her head is hanging to one side, but her head is held up as well with rope tied to the trunk. As if she's being forced to look at something, a few loose strands of hair frame her face. The rest of her hair is covered in mud.

It occurs to me that I had inadvertently touched her leg and swung it around. I gasp and run into Luke's arms, taking a few deep breaths to calm myself.

"What's wrong," he asks. When I turn to look at the tree, I realize that whoever did this knew exactly where to hide her from the trail.

The body is invisible, the ropes around her are hidden by the foliage. Unless you know exactly what to look for, you'd never spot her. I take his hand and lead him to where he can see. He covers his mouth with his hand as soon as he sees her.

He curses loudly, one word, and looks around at the way the body is positioned. From what I can see, I know that she has been here for some time decomposing slowly in a temperate rainforest at the tip of the Pacific Northwest.

"Who the hell did this?" Luke says under his breath.

I shake my head, forcing myself to look at her closer and begin the investigation by noting anything unusual even though I'm way out of my jurisdiction.

Despite how much I try to note the evidence and anything else that strikes me as peculiar about her, the only thing I can focus on are the ropes that are holding her up. The fact that someone had not just killed her but tied her up here to be found.

"We have to call someone," Luke says grabbing his phone.

"Of course," I nod.

I pick up mine and look at the bars. No reception. When I glance at his screen, he has none either.

"We have to head back out, call this in."

I give him a stern nod.

"Whoever did this," I say as we head back in an effort to find a few bars to make a call. "Whoever did this knew that he had time, that no one would come looking for him. This took a while, and he was confident that he wouldn't get caught."

"You think he'd done this before?"

"I almost guarantee it."

Chapter 11

When the local police show up at the scene, Detective Tony Mitchell is in the lead, charging in and staking his claim as if we're here looking for gold. He's a broad-shouldered, bald man, with the body of a retired linebacker who used to be fit but has somehow gained at least seventy pounds, eating the same way he did as a teenager. He's no stranger to intimidating people with his large size, but I'm used to working with all sorts of guys in a variety of law enforcement agencies and I will not let whatever intimidation I feel show on my face or in my posture.

He takes our statements, asking us banal questions, reviewing and double-checking our story separately. I don't find too many mistakes in his police work, but I hate his affect. Luke doesn't seem to be as bothered, given the fact that he works for the FBI and is used to people giving him attitude.

Whenever a case falls under the jurisdiction of the FBI, the local police are rarely happy to give up their turf. You get the credit for the cases that you solve. In fact, in the past, there had been a number of explosive situations that happened because the various law enforcement agencies did not share information among themselves. The most famous of which was of course the 9/11 bombers who flew airplanes into the World Trade Center.

After we have given our statements it begins to drizzle. Enough water falling to make you damp, but not enough to drive you to seek shelter. Sometimes the water would pool on the pines above, coming down as large, heavy drops that, for some reason, kept aiming straight for the back of my neck.

After a little while stomping my feet against the chill that seeped in through my hiking boots, the CSI team arrive and start collecting evidence from the body. I have looked at her as closely as I could while she was still tied to the tree, looking for the cause of death. There were no obvious strangulation marks around her neck and there were no bullet or stab wounds as far as I could see. I asked CSI for estimates of how long it had been since she'd died. Though they don't want to be put on the spot, one of them whispers that it looks like it might have been a couple of days.

"You know you're not investigating this case," Detective Mitchell comes over, practically pointing his finger in my face, or at least resisting the urge to.

"Excuse me?"

"I don't need you talking to our crime scene investigators."

"I'm just curious, that's all."

"You're a witness, not an investigator. This is my case to work."

"Look, I know I have no jurisdiction here. I'm just trying to be as helpful as possible."

"Nosy is more like it," he practically says under his breath.

I furrow my brow and whisper, "What the heck?" to Luke.

He just gives me a shrug and shakes his head. I've worked with a lot of moody cops who don't like to be questioned, but in this case, this guy seems to be coming out of left field completely.

What did we ever do to him to make him so pissed off? About half an hour later, I find out. His boss, Captain Carville arrives on the scene, a friendly older fellow, waving, who announces that he's going to be retiring this year and clearly can't wait to do so.

He's cheery, easygoing, but as soon as he

shows up, Detective Mitchell's mood shifts. It's like an act, a mask that he puts on. He smiles, acts friendly, and appears to be as cooperative as possible. When he disappears to use the bathroom, luckily a little bit of a walk away into the forest, I approach Captain Carville and ask him for a few minutes of his time. Not wanting to throw Detective Mitchell under the bus completely, I tiptoe around what I really want to ask.

"This is such an unusual case," I say. "Never seen anything like it. Have you?"

"Yes, it's definitely an odd one," he admits. "But there've been other cases. Not exactly like this, but similar enough."

"Really?" I ask. "In Olympia?"

He nods.

"Unfortunately, we haven't had much luck in tying all the pieces together. I don't know if you got that sense from Detective Mitchell."

I tilt my head and lean forward. I'm drenched at this point, my shirt is completely soaked through. The drizzle is still not a full-blown rainfall, but all the little droplets have added up and I'm soaked.

"There're a few unsolved cases that we've been working. I'm not sure if this woman fits into it or not, but the last few have not gone so well for Detective Mitchell and he's a little on edge."

"Oh, okay. That explains it. He was short with

me. I just don't want him to think that I'm trying to step on any toes here."

"No, it's not you. He's been like that for a while. I really hope that this doesn't just add to the pile of cold cases because it's not going to make the department look good."

It sounds like he is a little bit too focused on the department, rather than the victim and what it means for their family. But I know where he's coming from. You say stuff like that to not get into the personal stuff too much. You just want to keep everything professional. Give yourself space to avoid being overwhelmed with all this darkness.

"I don't know you very well, Ms. Carr, but I just want to ask you a favor that I probably have no right to ask, but I want you to cut him a little bit of slack. Besides the unsolved homicides, there's just been a bunch of overdoses, suicides in the department, that kind of thing, and it's really been taking a toll. It's usually that time of year when things like this increase around here. The rain just keeps on falling. People get depressed. But it feels different this time. I really don't know why, but it just does."

"Yes, I understand," I say, giving him a knowing nod.

"The thing is that there're seasons and patterns to things. Maybe things don't align perfectly, but just like with retail, for instance, when they try to go all in the black by Black Friday and make most of their profit between the end of November and Christmas. There are times of year when suicides are up, along with murders and drug overdoses."

When the crime scene investigators are ready to take the body down, we stand aside and give them space, watching carefully. I look for bullet wounds, blood coming in and out. We don't see anything from the way that they lower her.

Just because the strangulation marks around the neck are not obvious doesn't mean that she wasn't strangled, but bruising being what it is, it does generally show up.

"How do you think she was killed?" I ask Captain Carville.

"Drugs. Suffocated with something. There're so many different ways to go. It's hard to tell."

I nod. So does Luke.

"Will you give me a call?" I ask him. "Just when you find out more and let me know if there's anything else we can do."

"Of course." He nods. "And you didn't see anyone when you were here?" He asks even though we have answered this several times already.

I shake my head. "No, sorry."

"It seems like CSI thinks that she's been here for some time."

"Yes. I mean, it's possible, but she was hanging right there," I say. "If you walk back and forth, you won't be able to see her unless you know what to look for."

"Knowing that, however, doesn't make this job much easier, does it?" Captain Carville says.

Chapter 12

I have plans to meet up with Donald and Mary Lou again the following morning, but I go by myself. Luke has a bad migraine, stays in bed, and I promise that we're going to go do a little bit of sight-seeing or at least go to dinner to try to get our mind off things. I arrive at Donald's house when the sun is just peeking out through the clouds. It hasn't been raining this morning, but it's still overcast and gray, making the pines all around his property look almost menacing.

Mary Lou is as peppy as ever, inviting me out back for a brunch that she had prepared. I apologize again that Luke isn't there, and she quickly takes his plate away and tells me not to worry about it. We sit at the outside table, and I regret not bringing a sweater because it's not as warm as both of them seem to think it is. Maybe it's just because I've been spoiled by Southern California.

"I have given what you said some thought," I say. I keep the body from yesterday to myself for now, still uncertain as to whether I want to go into all of that. I'm here to clear my mind, think about something else. "I don't understand why you need my help."

Mary Lou brings out a caprese salad, gives it one quick swirl with a knife and fork. I take a sip of my lemonade. I feel uncomfortable talking about gruesome bodies and death at a time like this.

Donald, on the other hand, seems to have no problem. He even has his packet of manila folders with whatever evidence that he believes he has right next to him. I eye it from time to time as I try a hunk of Mary Lou's garlic bread and, as it melts in my mouth, I decide to just come right out and tell him.

"I don't know what you think I'm capable of that the local law enforcement isn't, but I don't see how I can help you in this situation."

"Look, I know that last time I put a lot on you," he says, draining the last of his beer and then quickly getting another one. "But don't you think I have compelling evidence? A guy in prison telling me that stuff about his uncle? That's a lot."

"Then why don't other investigators jump in on that?"

"Because they think it's fruit of the poisonous tree. They don't believe me. They think I'm a nut. There's only so far I can go with this."

"I'm a stranger here, you need someone local. I don't have any jurisdiction."

"You would be a private investigator," he says. "Just asking questions."

"Can you just tell me about my dad without this?”

Donald tilts his head. His demeanor changes. He swallows hard and looks at me. "I wish I could."

Mary Lou brings out the soup and no matter how much he tries to lift the spirits at the table, everything is different now. I'm shivering, partly from the cold and partly from the discomfort with the brunch. I don't want to be here. This feels a lot like he's trying to get me to do something that I don't want to do, but I'm not exactly certain about what move to make.

"Can I tell you more? Can I show you pictures?"

I give him a slight nod. He pulls out the manila folder.

"This is Victor McFadden. This is the guy who's in prison. His wife killed his child, and he was in the midst of committing a large fraud against the government that they only found out after the murder and started going through all their paperwork."

"You worked this case?" I ask.

"Yes, I did. Despite what he did, I feel sorry for him. He got a crappy hand, so we connected. Everything is true, just like I told you before. I just want you to see his face."

A man looks up at me. The photo that was taken is against a pale wall somewhere in the prison. It's the two of them together. Victor is a tall, lanky guy with auburn hair and high cheekbones. There's nothing particularly distinctive about him or that interesting. He just looks like a guy serving time in a white-collar prison.

"I don't know what you want me to do with this. I mean, yes, I see the picture of him."

"This is his uncle." He shows me a picture of an overweight, pudgy guy with some similar characteristics like the high cheekbones similar to Victor. His name is David Trincia. He's wearing thick glasses and has a receding hairline.

"Okay, this is the guy that you suspect?" I ask.

"Yes, this is him. I followed him a few times, but he lost me. I don't know if he knew that I was following him or what happened exactly."

"I see the pictures, Donald, but I don't know what you want."

"I want you to help me."

"How?"

"Follow him. I want you to follow him."

"And do what? Do you think he's going to commit a crime or murder when I'm around? I mean, what am I following him to do? While he's running errands, going to Costco, filling his prescriptions? What's the point?"

"Okay. If you don't believe me, why don't you go talk to Victor? I'm sure that he can get you on the list to the prison."

"Let's assume he's going to tell me the same story that you said," I say, giving him the most benefit of the doubt. "Let's just assume that."

"Isn't that good enough?"

"No, it's not," I put my fork down. "I'm done pretending that any of this makes sense. You say you know things about my father, right? Just tell me what they are. And if you refuse to, then how can I ever trust you? I mean, you're blackmailing me here to work this case that I don't even know if it's a real case at all."

"Listen, why don't you two take a break?" Mary Lou interrupts. "Come here, Kaitlyn. I want to talk to you in private."

I'm glad that she has separated us. The tensions were starting to run high, and I was starting to feel like I was going to blow. Inside their house, she takes me to what is probably her office. One side of it is all bookshelves, the other is lined with desks covered with craft supplies and artwork.

"Did you paint these?" I ask, pointing to the wall. There's an abstract piece with many different colors all mixed together, resembling something of a wave.

"Yes, it's called acrylic pour painting. Very thin paint, we pour it on one after another and it turns out how it turns out, kind of hard to control."

"Do you do it right here?" I ask, pointing to the new textured carpet that looks pristine.

"Yes. It's difficult. I've got to cover the whole floor up, otherwise it will get everywhere. I'm not sure that this technique is for me, it's a little too messy. But I like how some of the pieces turned out. I'm mostly into pottery though."

I look at her books, a mixture of romances and thrillers as well as some award-winning literary fiction.

"You read everything, huh?"

She nods. "Yes. I don't like to discriminate. Whatever sounds interesting, strikes my fancy, I go with it."

"That's good," I say.

"I have to tell you about my husband. He can be intense. He's been working these cases for a long time, and probably to his detriment, but he thinks he's getting somewhere."

"Thinks? You don't agree?"

She shrugs.

"I used to, but sometimes you just have to accept that certain cases perhaps can't be solved."

"So, you don't have that much faith in him?"

"No, I do. What I'm trying to say is that I didn't. For a long time, it seemed like he was just going after anything and everything, but then this man in prison came along and they got close, and he mentioned something. I know that he's pressing you too much, and I can see you're pushing away, but it doesn't mean that he's wrong. I thought it was a long shot, but when we went through the evidence, it really lines up, Kaitlyn."

"Look, it may line up for you, but it's just not for me. I don't have any superpowers to solve these cases that are impossible all on my own. You have to work with the authorities. They have the resources."

"Will you at least look at what he has, the case file itself?"

"Perhaps," I shrug. "I just hate the way that he's going about it. It's like he's keeping this information about my father hostage or something to try to get me to do what, exactly, work with him?"

"Yes. If he can accept your word, he will," she says. "If you promise to help him, he'll tell you about your father sooner rather than later."

I take a deep breath, and then I realize that there is a black cat sitting in the recliner in the corner. I only spot the green of his eyes when he blinks. Seeing that I had spotted him, Mary Lou smiles, walks over, and gives him a little rub behind the ears.

"This is Douglas," she says.

"That's a cute name. May I pet him?"

She nods as I approach. The cat doesn't move, and when I give him a pet, he starts to purr.

"Douglas is a rescue and he's named after John Douglas, the FBI agent who profiled the most notorious serial killers in history."

"You mean Ted Bundy, Jeffrey Dahmer, and the BTK killer?" I ask.

"Yes. Just to name a few. He helped drag down the worst predators around and we, for one, especially Donald, we hold him in great esteem for the work that he had done."

"Look, I know it's a big deal, the work that Donald's doing, and I appreciate it, but sometimes there's just not enough."

"But you don't know that," she says. "You don't know what is enough and what isn't. You haven't looked at the evidence and that's all I want you to do, is just take a look and let me know what you think."

"Is that all he wants me to do? Because he hasn't offered up the files at all. He wants me to make all these commitments."

"I can talk to him. We can negotiate. Will you

come back to finish brunch? I have a really great apple pie that I made from scratch that I just know that you're going to love."

I take a deep breath in and nod.

"Okay," I say. "Let's do that."

Chapter 13

The following day, I find out the identity of the missing woman. Her name is Cora Leonelle and she was a hairdresser and stylist at Hair Bliss Salon. She had one son who was in 10th grade, and he was the one who had reported her missing that evening, or at least tried to, but the operator wouldn't take his call. Cora had been missing for ten days and due to the fact that the cameras in the parking lot at the trailhead weren't working at the time when she was taken there by the killer, the investigation had pretty much stalled.

Captain Carville asked me to come in to speak to him again, give another statement, and Luke as well. I don't see much of a point, but I cooperate as much as I can. Maybe they'll give me some more information about her.

The station is nondescript like so many others

that I've been to. Nothing really to catch your attention, except for one of the detectives sitting in the back with a giant bouquet of flowers on her desk. She looks almost embarrassed when I comment on them and tell her that they're beautiful. I know exactly how she feels. She tells me that they're from her boyfriend, a guy that she's recently started seeing, but he doesn't work in law enforcement.

While most women would love to get a giant bouquet of flowers, this display of affection can be embarrassing for a woman working for the police department. The problem is that most men there put you in a special box as a *female* cop or a *female* detective, and are usually not the type to give flowers to their girlfriends and wives. Drawing attention to yourself and your sex, and the fact that you might enjoy something like this tends to make you a little bit uncomfortable.

Captain Carville shows me to his office, a sign of respect more than anything, rather than taking me to one of the interrogation rooms. Luke is going to stop by a little later because it's not good to interview people at the same time.

I'm under no illusion that this is anything but an interview. He asks for more details. I provide as much as I can. Anything that would strike me as important. He asks me to describe the people we saw on the way. Those are harder to remember. We had nodded to a few here and there.

"Was it a woman, a man?"

"Both. More than two. I don't know."

I give him my best educated guess. After my statement is reviewed, he lets out a big sigh.

"Can you tell me more about the victim?" I ask.

"Sure. She was getting ready to go on a date. We found this out later when we talked to her son. He had no idea that she'd started seeing this friend of hers. According to him, they were going to be making it official with her son and his girlfriend."

"Like introducing them?"

"No. They had met," Captain Carville says, tapping his pen on the table. It's a nervous habit that I'm all too familiar with. He finishes a cup of coffee and asks if I want another. I decline and he seems mildly annoyed because he clearly wants one but doesn't want to leave to get one for himself.

"So, she was going to introduce her friend as her new boyfriend to her son?"

"Yes. He was going to pick her up from her work."

"And she was going to leave her car there?" I ask.

"She didn't have her car. He drove her to

work. They'd been spending a lot of time together."

"And who is this guy?"

He looks at his paperwork. "Steven Hildebrand. There were friends for a while. Friends of a friend, they had just started dating. He had owned an auto mechanic shop and had sold it to a chain. Had enough for a retirement," he said.

"Wow, how old is he?"

"43. He said he stayed around because this relationship had started. He really loved her. Seemed distraught."

"What do you mean stayed around?" I ask.

"Not that many people dream of retiring in wet and soggy Olympia, Washington, as you may suspect. We all have plans of going down to Palm Springs, Arizona, Sunbelt, the usual suspects."

"Yes. I looked at some of your home prices and it's actually cheaper down there," I say.

"How do you handle the heat?"

"You get used to it. The late part of the summer is monsoon season. It can be humid and overcast, but not 115, so it's nice."

"Glad to hear that."

"Oh, yes, that's right. You're retiring."

Suddenly his whole face lights up. It's like with one word all the sadness and all the pressure of the job have been wiped away.

"Counting down the days."

"How many exactly?"

"78."

"This year," I say. "How does it feel?"

"I can't wait. It's freaking amazing. My wife has already rented the condo. We're headed to Phoenix and we're going to stay there for a bit. We have our RV and plan to travel around the Southwest, see where we want to settle, see where we meet people."

"RVing would be awesome."

"Yes, maybe we'll do that for a bit. Just going to be amazing. Last winter here, that's for sure."

"I'm glad to hear that. I mean, most people only dream of retirement."

"How about you?" he asks. "How much time do you have?"

"13 years until I get to twenty."

"That's the golden number, isn't it? You started earlier," he says. "Those guys that start at 21, they have it made, don't they?"

"I guess."

"I'm here pushing 60," he says. "I can't say the job has been terrible the whole time. Benefits are good, pay is good, especially overtime when the city can swing it."

"Are things more difficult now?"

"No, there's plenty of overtime just not that many people working. A little bit too much. I got to assign people crazy shifts like never before.

With everything that the departments have gone through, we're lucky that we didn't have everyone quit all at once like that one department in North Carolina."

"I guess they were just trying to make a statement that they didn't like the new captain."

"And I thought I had trouble coming in," he says.

"I'm sorry it's been tough."

"Hey, I'm the one that's sorry for dumping all this on you. You're here on vacation, right?"

"Well, actually no, not exactly."

I figured that Captain Carville had shared so much with me that maybe it's my turn to share a little bit of what I'm going through as well.

He tilts his head. "You're not here for something bad that has happened that's personal. Right?"

"Kind of, yes." I nod. "Since we've sort of connected now, I was wondering if maybe I could run this past you, get an outsider's point of view."

"Okay," he says.

"Well, I got a call out of the blue from this retired FBI agent. It was a known thing that my father had committed suicide. I mean I suspected there was more to it. When I came home, my mom had found him, he shot himself in the stomach. I thought that was a very cruel, difficult way to die and that anyone who's been in law enforcement would not exactly choose that over blowing your head off, right?"

He nods.

"Sorry, I don't mean to be so crude. It's just that I've talked about this plenty with my mom and with the police and I've gone over this and read so many reports that I feel like I'm going nuts."

"Okay, keep going."

"I met with a partner of his. He convinced me that it was suicide. I mean, he had a compelling story about what my Dad had been involved with. He was selling drugs, he was an informant."

"Anyway, for many years I thought that someone else was involved, that it was a murder. My mom didn't. I talked to this guy from the local police department in Big Bear and he agreed with my mom, and I put the whole thing to bed. I thought, fine. That's what happened. This was many years ago, by the way. But then out of the blue I get this letter from an FBI agent from up here. He says that he has more information about my father and he says he needs my help to work on some cold cases that the cops and the FBI are refusing to help him with. He claims he is going to tell me what happened to my father, but he won't tell me yet, only after I help him. He says that he has compelling evidence. Somebody, a witness from prison. I don't know what I'm supposed to do with that information, I mean not really."

When I say that, I see the way that his face drops just a little. I tilt my head toward him and ask, "Do you know who I'm talking about?"

He pauses for a moment. "Would it happen to be Donald C. Clark?"

Chapter 14

When I say his name, Captain Carville's face changes expression. That sharp attention returns that had vanished when we talked about his retirement and I can tell that he's agitated, annoyed.

"You know him?" I ask.

"Of course, I know him. He's been talking to every cop in the Pacific Northwest, trying to get anyone to listen."

"He's what, a nut?"

"Yes, that's one way of putting it. Conspiracy theorist, lost soul, someone who needs to get the hell out of this rainy region and get himself some vitamin D. Maybe that'll improve his mood."

"What are you saying exactly?"

"He was forced into early retirement by the FBI. He was obsessed with these cold cases. He thought that they were connected to the same serial killer. There's no proof. Even though the evidence doesn't line up, and the modus operandi, and all the manners of death are completely different, he still keeps harping on the fact that they're connected. You know how police investigations work, you have to put the pieces together. You can't just have a hunch, a hunch can sometimes lead you somewhere, but just as often it can get you fitting evidence to your theory instead of the other way around."

"Tell me what's going on with him," I say, not wanting a lecture on police reporting.

"He came around," the Captain continues. "He made his case here to me after the FBI basically got sick of him. He wasn't working his other cases; he was just working on this phantom serial killer. There're a lot of cold cases out here. I hate to say it, but there just are. We have acres and acres of deep, dense forest. You saw where that body was found. Unless you're walking there, and you're looking exactly where you looked, you would have missed it. How many other people had walked by that exact same spot over the last ten days that she's been missing? Who knows? The foliage is thick. The rains wash away evidence. It's a perfect place to bury bodies, or to leave them somewhere where no one will find them.

"This isn't a very heavily populated place. This

isn't Seattle, or anywhere like that. Then on top of all that, you have animals who'll scavenge and destroy all the evidence. All that together leaves a lot of cases unsolved. Donald found some that he believes are connected. He's retired and unfortunately now has 24 hours a day to devote to his theories. Somehow I guess he found some leverage to get you involved."

"That's difficult to hear. He seemed so normal."

"That's what he has going for him. I'm not saying that he's 100% wrong, I don't know that, but he goes on these wild goose chases, and he hasn't solved a homicide or even a crime for years. That's why the FBI asked him to leave. He just wasn't working on the cases that he was supposed to, and he was obsessed with this one."

"What about this informant?" I ask.

"He worked with a couple," Captain Carville says. "There's the one who said that he knew who did it; led him on for about a year. Nothing happened, didn't know anything. Finally admitted it but Donald doesn't believe it. He thinks that he was scared to death to reveal who it is and just stopped talking. Then there was this guy that he put away. His wife had killed his child and he had defrauded the government for millions. Now he's doing time in a white-collar prison, and he's bored, at least that's what I think it is. Nobody's visiting him. He has no family. To keep him around, he's telling him some stories. What are the chances of it being his uncle?"

The fact that Captain Carville knows so much about this case makes me feel uncomfortable. It means that he has gone to almost everyone before coming to me.

"My guess is that he looked you and a bunch of other people up, and he tried to find some way to compel you to come up here. Maybe he read an article or did some research about your father and figured it's an unsolved case. That might get you into it. That's my guess. I wouldn't waste your time on it. Unless, of course, you have some lingering questions about your father, but then you have to ask yourself, does Donald actually have answers? And why would he?"

I leave the precinct with a sense of confusion and uncertainty. I had certain feelings about Donald Clark and his theories, but now they appear to have been justified. I walk back to my car feeling conflicted. I'm not one for conspiracy theories, but I also don't ignore evidence and statements just because they come from a source that isn't entirely trustworthy.

This often leads me down a rabbit hole, which

is difficult to get out of. The main thing that is a cause for concern when it comes to Donald is, of course, the fact that instead of simply asking me for help, he got me up here under false pretenses, or at least what appear to be false pretenses.

He had assumed that I wouldn't want to help and used my father as leverage, but in thinking this, am I making certain assumptions as well? One being that he had found me in a list of detectives who he could influence by using my father's mysterious death in that manner.

I drive out of the precinct and get on the highway. Driving past strip malls, I let my mind wander. Can any of this be true or is Donald just taking me for a fool? Someone who is an outsider who would spend time helping him work his case and participate in I guess what some would call delusion in order to get someone to believe in him? The thing about having beliefs is that you need people to participate in your theory in order to make it become real.

Obviously, having people on your side who have a certain amount of credibility goes a long way as well. Without a cop like me or another detective or an FBI agent, it's just him.

He has been working this case long enough to realize that very few people seem to believe him and not because they don't want to. The thing about cops is that, most of the time, we want to believe.

We want to solve the case. We are the right audience. We are the choir to be preached to.

We want to look, we want the things to connect and for stories to come together and for it all to make sense because, well, it's our job to solve the case and so if all these people have rejected his theory, what does that mean?

What does it say about it? That there's very little evidence to go on and there's very little point in even going forward with it.

That's probably why he reached out to me.

That's probably why he entangled my father in this whole story, because why else would I even be here if he hadn't dangled that carrot in front of me?

"Help me with the case and I'll help you find out what happened to your father. Or better yet, I'll show you what I have. These files you'll have the answers you're seeking. If only you promise to help me in return."

As I drive, I become filled with a sense of resentment. He used me and he wasted my time. I came up here for nothing. The whole thing is made up. I become more and more certain of that fact, the more I think about it and the way that he has gone about getting my help.

If he had had evidence about my father, why

hadn't he reached out before? Why let it just be the way it was? He was fine with me never knowing the truth until he needed something from me and then suddenly it was a big deal. Suddenly my father's death was this mysterious murder that needed to be solved.

When, in reality, it was just a plain old suicide with no mystery whatsoever. Just a lot of pain and heartache.

I should wait for Luke to come with me. I know that, but I still drive to Donald's house by myself. I knock slightly and then try the knob. It's open and I let myself in.

"Donald! Mary Lou!" I yell.

Donald comes out of his study. I'm still standing on the threshold, clenching my jaw.

None of this is prepared. None of this is planned.

"Hey, you're back," he says with cheer.

"I'm back because I had a little chat with somebody. Somebody that you have talked to as well, I guess enough times to annoy him."

"Who?"

"Captain Carville," I say, "with the Olympia Police Department."

His Adam's apple moves up and down, keeping his frustration at bay.

"Why were you talking to him?" he asks after a long pause.

"Luke and I went on a walk. We found a body and called it in. We started talking and he asked me why I was here. I told him about this case. Much to my surprise, he knew all about you."

"You knew that I was working on these cases and that means that I talk to the local law enforcement agencies. I didn't hide anything from you," Donald insists.

"Yes, but he went so far as to tell me that there's nothing really to it. You're trying to make a case out of nothing, trying to connect impossible dots to one another. In fact, the FBI thought that too. They asked you to retire early, didn't they? Because you were spending so much time looking for a phantom serial killer."

"He's real and those people are really dead," Donald says, clenching his jaw and speaking through his teeth.

"I think you manipulated me," I say. "I think you needed help, you wanted someone from law enforcement on your side and so you probably wrote a bunch of different letters to different cops. Was I the only sob story you could find or were there more? Maybe I'm the only one that took the bait, the only one stupid enough, huh?"

"That's not what happened, and you know it."

"How do I know?" I snap. "I don't know anything. You're keeping secrets from me."

"I have the files right here, you can take them."

"They're files of your interviews with the guy in prison who just needs a friend to talk to. This isn't supernatural, Donald, this is just what happens. You showed an interest, and he's giving you what you want. There was another informant, right? The one who didn't work out?"

He looks away from me.

"Of course, there was," I say. "I know it as much as you do."

Chapter 15

Donald and I go in circles. Whatever tension that Marylou had diffused earlier is back with a vengeance. He has lied to me, exaggerated, not been completely truthful, whatever you want to call it, and I'm angry and pissed off. I start to walk away. This isn't headed in a good direction.

Then he grabs my arm and says, "I want to show you something. It's about your father."

He leads me back to his office and I stand impatiently with my arms crossed, tapping my foot on the floor while he rifles through numerous pieces of paper and manila folders looking for something.

Finally, he finds a CD-ROM and puts it into his ancient computer. It feels like the technology in this room is over a decade, if not two, old. What shows up on screen is a closed-circuit recording, black and white, of two men talking in a motel room.

"I need you to take him out," one of them says after Donald fast-forwards a little bit through the video.

They're sitting opposite each other on two couches with a small coffee table in the middle. The room is filled with debris, discarded cups, and beer bottles. Somewhere in the distance, there is an unmade bed.

"I'm not going to take him out. He's an informant," the other guy says.

The audio and the video are both grainy but clear enough to understand what is being said.

"You have to make it look like a suicide," the guy on the left says, "like he has shot himself in the gut."

"How am I supposed to do that?" the guy with the receding hairline asks.

"You threaten him. You threaten his family. You make him do it or you and your family are dead. You better not go to the cops either, they're going to suspect something is wrong."

Receding hairline guy says, "No, they won't. He's depressed. He drinks too much. He talks about suicide a lot. He's no good, and a criminal. He feels bad about that, unlike most of them out there."

My throat closes up. They're talking about my

father and yet, they haven't said his name. I listen closely. I let my arms fall to my sides.

"David Carr. You take him out and you make it look like a suicide. I'll pay you the money that I owe you," the thinner guy on the other couch says, pointing his finger in his partner's face.

"Why? Why do I have to do this?"

"Because he's going to turn. He's going to work with the cops against us. He's already working with them. He hasn't told them everything, but he's going to tell them about us."

"What if he doesn't?"

"Listen, you do this, you help me or we're through. It's him or you, his family or yours. If I have to go and do all of this myself, then I'm going to make you pay for it. I'm going to make you suffer."

After that point, the audio recording gets very grainy. My breath gets stuck in the back of my throat and I feel like someone has punched me in the stomach. I fold over in half, uncertain as to where to go from here.

"I told you that I know about your father. Do you believe me now?" Donald asks.

I turn and look up at him. I'm sitting on the back of my ankles with my arms wrapped around my knees.

Who is this man and what does he know?

"We were working a case," he says, as if reading my mind. "It was an unrelated case, we had a tail on this guy on the left, the one who made the threat. We had no idea how he was involved with anything else. Then all of a sudden, we have the camera up in his motel room and there he is making this threat."

"Why didn't you stop him?"

"We told your father that someone was going to come after him. A lot of the information was confidential, ongoing investigation and all, but I went over personally to talk to him. I told him that someone was going to come and threaten him and try to get him to take his own life. I told him who it was."

"Who was it?"

He hesitates for a moment.

"Max Powell. He was a higher up in a cartel, but he was going out on his own. We were investigating him on the string of murders related to his line of work. A warning was all I could do for your father. He wasn't my concern at that time. Once he knew he was expecting someone to come, he knew he had to be prepared, but he didn't tell anyone. He didn't tell the local precinct; he didn't take any precautions when it came to you, or your mother, or your sister. I don't know why."

"He just what, accepted his fate?" I ask.

"Maybe."

"Are you saying that he wanted to get killed?"

"No, I'm not saying that at all. The fact that he had a weapon there probably means that he was going to try and protect himself, but we were working a different case. We were trying to take down the cartel, for Christ's sake, but I still felt bad and lost. I wasn't sure where to go with all of this. You don't believe me about the serial killer? Fine. I thought you would help me, but I want you to know that I'm a stand-up guy that I'm telling you the truth. I could be wrong about some stuff and maybe I got you up here under the wrong pretenses. Perhaps I was wrong, but I wanted to tell you this anyway and I thought you could help me in return."

"Where are these guys?" I ask. "The ones that came for my dad."

"I don't know that. Max Powell disappeared. We were trailing him, building a case, and then poof."

"Are you saying someone killed him?"

"There're a lot of people who end up with their heads cut off who work for the Mexican cartels. That could've been his fate."

"Or?" I ask.

"Or he took the money that he made and

disappeared himself. They told me they were removing me from the case. There was enough evidence. We got a few lower-level guys, but that's it."

Chapter 16

The conversation with Donald leaves me heartbroken. If I hadn't seen the video for myself, with Max Powell calling my father by name, I probably wouldn't have believed him. But the video was so clear. It explained why there was a gunshot wound to my father's stomach. It explained why he had to suffer. He was there trying to protect us in whatever capacity that he could. Maybe he should have done more, should have sent us away, should have fled himself, but the details of that night continue to be so murky to me.

I haven't been back to Big Bear Lake since my sister's disappearance. I've talked to her on the phone a lot and promised to come back, but work got busy, and time slipped away. That small mountain town, with the little statues of carved wooden bears all over the place, it's so quaint on the outside. Yet just below the surface, there's darkness brewing, secrets and lies everywhere. Mostly surrounding my family.

I thought I had put everything to bed. I thought that I could move forward. My family no longer had any secrets, but this situation with my father just opens up a whole host of uncertainty and mystery, questions that I'm not entirely sure I want to ask. I don't know if I'm prepared for the answers.

As soon as I get back to the hotel and see Luke, I burst into tears. I can barely get a hold of myself and end up gasping for breath, trying to tell him what has happened. A good hour passes before I get my story fully out and I'm able to speak normally, even though tears still come and go occasionally. Through my overflow of emotion he somehow puts the story together.

"Your father committed suicide," he says. "It was a known fact. You've confirmed it with the guy from Fawnskin, his partner."

"Yes. I know that except that, I guess, he didn't know the whole story. He knew parts of it. I saw the video, Luke," I say, wiping the rest of the moisture off my face. "It was these two guys talking about killing my father. Max Powell, the thinner one on the left is the one who demanded that he be executed, and for it to look like a suicide. He threatened the other guy."

"What was his name?"

"Deacon Omni."

It takes me a minute to remember his name, because Donald had only mentioned it at the very end.

"He had threatened Deacon's family. He told him that if he didn't do it, then he would be the one who ended up dead. Then, what happened to him afterwards, Donald doesn't know. They looked for him everywhere, but he disappeared. He says there're two options, the cartel took him out, or he left on his own, hiding out somewhere under a different identity. He knows how to do that. He was a higher up. He had changed his identity often. Then Donald was assigned to a different case, and nothing happened."

"What about the guy who supposedly did it?"

A lump forms in the back of my throat. I try to take a few deep breaths and calm down.

"That's the thing. They never went anywhere with it. Donald had reached out personally to my father, warned him about it, told him to take us away and to go away himself. I guess he didn't think that this was a real threat. Donald said that he got his life threatened all the time, but isn't it a big deal when an FBI agent comes and shows up like this?" I add. "I mean, shouldn't he have taken him more seriously, and why didn't he go to the police?"

"It seems to me that Donald was working by himself at this point," Luke says. "He probably went off script by contacting your father, and he couldn't very well reach out to the cops."

"Why didn't my dad take him seriously? Why did he just pretend that it was going to be okay?"

"I don't know."

I bury my head in Luke's shoulder and cry. All these emotions, the regret and devastation that I had buried somewhere deep inside comes bursting to the surface. I thought I had grieved my father properly, but now I wasn't sure what had happened at all, and the grief I thought I'd dealt with came right back up. The sadness had mixed itself up with anger that I could only point at Donald.

"He still had no right to coerce me into working with him."

"No, of course not," Luke agrees, "but I wonder how much he worried about your reaction and how dealing with what had happened with your father and all the unknowns involved with that might take your attention from what he wants, which is to solve his case."

"Why did he tell me this now? I demand to know. I mean, why did he just dump this all in my lap?"

"Because you showed up there, you talked to the captain, you confronted him. I guess he figured he's lost you anyway. So you might as well know about your father."

"Do you think that's what happened?" I ask.

He gives me a slight nod.

"Well, I'm not going to work with him after what he has done. He should have just come forward."

"Yes, I agree," he says, "and I guess he knows that to some extent."

I grit my teeth. I hate the predicament that I find myself in. He's asking me now, he's no longer pushing me, trying to influence me. Now, I owe him a favor, which is perhaps worse than what was happening before. It is still a manipulation, just a different emotional wedge.

Feeling a little bit more at peace, Luke pulls away. I pull away from him and lay down with my head on the pillow, staring at the ceiling.

"Are you hungry?" Luke asks, turning on the TV, mindlessly flipping through the channels.

I grab my phone, check my email, and read the local news. I'm tempted to look up every name I know, every name that he had listed. Max Powell, Deacon Omni, Victor McFadden, and David Trincia. It's also nice to just lie here and do nothing in particular. He asks me again if I want lunch and we go through the menus of the local restaurants that can deliver to the hotel.

"Let's just go downstairs," I say. "There's probably a good enough place down there. The menu looks fine."

As I gather my things, I use the bathroom and look at myself in the mirror realizing that I'm in no position to go out. My eyes are puffy, makeup completely smeared. I splash some water on my face, but it's no better.

"Listen, do you mind if we just get room service?" I ask. "I want to just get into my pajamas and curl up under the covers for a bit."

"Yes, no problem," he says.

He places our order on the room phone and thirty minutes later, there is a knock on the door. Luke is in the bathroom, so I force myself to get out of bed. When I open the door, I see a lanky teenager standing before me with no room service cart in sight.

Chapter 17

"Do you have the food?" I ask the young man standing before me.

He looks at me blankly. His hair is poofy and curly, like a mop on top of his head. He's dressed in an oversized smiley face T-shirt and loose, white-washed jeans. Then it occurs to me that he is not here to deliver the food.

"Can I help you?" I ask. "Are you looking for a specific room?"

"I'm looking for Detective Kaitlyn Carr," he says, looking straight at me with his piercing blue eyes.

"That's me. You are?"

"I'm Anthony Leonelle," he says. "You were the one who found my mom up on Lost Creek Trail."

My mouth drops open. I pause, not knowing

what to say. When Luke comes out, he introduces himself and Anthony, again, repeats what he has just told me word for word.

"That was your mom up there?" I ask, showing him into our messy hotel room. I immediately try to cover up the unmade bed.

I look like a wreck. My hair is down, unbrushed. I had just toweled it off and let it dry after getting wet in the rain. I'm wearing an oversized sweatshirt and mismatched sweatpants to boot, but Anthony doesn't seem to care. I take all our papers off of the dining room table by the window and offer him a seat. He takes it. I'm about to sit on the edge of the bed when Luke points to the chair across from Anthony and takes a seat on the bed himself.

"How did you find me?" I ask.

"I was talking to the detective," he says, looking down and picking at something on the table. "He mentioned that a detective had found her there. I wasn't supposed to find out your name, but he left me with the paperwork for a minute and I searched. It had your address listed at this hotel. Are you visiting the area for a little bit?"

"Yes. Just here on a work trip," I say. "We went hiking and that's how I found her."

"Can you tell me anything else?" he asks.

“The detectives aren’t saying anything, and I just feel like they're keeping something from me."

"I'm not sure what I could say."

I bite my lower lip. I go through my story of what had happened and how I spotted her. He nods looking down, cracking his knuckles.

"Why are you here, Anthony?" I ask.

"The police ignored my calls that night. I tried to report her missing. They said that I should call back the next day, because it had only been a couple of hours. I told them that it wasn’t like her. She would never not get back to me. They kept stalling, saying that maybe she’d lost her phone or forgot and that I had to give it more time, that they were short-staffed. They just didn't care about her right from the beginning and now she's dead."

Tears well up in his eyes. He breaks down a little bit. I stand up and put my arm around him. I want to make it better, but I don't know how.

"Why are you here, Anthony?" I ask again.

"I need your help," he says, choking back tears, wiping his face with the back of his arm. "I don't have anyone. Dad doesn't care about her because they got divorced and he has a new family."

"Is there something that you think I should know about her boyfriend?" I ask.

He shakes his head forward. "I didn't know

that she had a boyfriend but apparently, she'd started seeing this friend of hers. They interviewed him and said that he wasn't a suspect, but I can't believe them. They lied to me so much and they never cared. Since you found her and since you're a detective yourself, maybe you can help me. Maybe you can talk to that guy."

"Can you tell me more about him? What's his name?"

"Steven Hildebrand. He lives at 1611 4th Avenue E. I was going to go talk to him myself, and I did a little bit, but maybe you can too."

My trip to the Pacific Northwest has gotten infinitely more complicated. When I look up Steven Hildebrand's address on my phone, I see that his house is less than a 15-minute drive away. I don't have much of a reason not to talk to him. The boy who came to see me is lost, confused, and desperately missing his mother. He had been notified that she was found dead, murdered, displayed in the most precarious way. He had searched for her for ten days.

He was lucky that she was found at all. The killer had put her up there, in that particular place, not to be found, or at least, not to be found soon. Of course, he could have buried her, taken her further into the woods if he really wanted to hide her body, but he didn't. He wanted her to be found, but only after the elements had ensured that all traces of who had done it were hidden. Given where she was located, I doubt that he was dumb enough to leave DNA evidence or any other kind of evidence either for that matter.

Unless, of course, it got there by accident. He may not have known that there was no camera surveillance available at that time. He also felt confident enough in the area, to carry her there, and tie her up high on the tree using probably a ladder of some sort since she was positioned quite high. Nevertheless, as much as I would like to put this case behind me and just be a witness, happy that I could be of some service in locating the body. Anthony's pleas come back to me. He's tortured and sad.

Given the fact that he had lived with his mom the majority of his life and that they were so close, my heart really goes out to him. There're not that many teenage sons who would call their mother one of their best friends. Looking at their social media, I can see why. They had done 5Ks together. He participated in a number of charity events at her salon, the majority benefiting multiple sclerosis. There are numerous pictures of them in an embrace at family barbecues and of her coloring his hair.

What takes me by surprise then is that she didn't tell him about her boyfriend. Perhaps, she wanted to keep something to herself or maybe she was just waiting for the right time. I decide to just go by the boyfriend's place, scope it out, see how I feel about talking to him when I get there.

Along the road, leading into the neighborhood, I find a coffee stand, just a little cabin, positioned all by itself in the middle of a parking lot. Cars pull over and get takeout from it. It's not exactly a drive-through because there's nowhere else to enter. I pull up and order a cappuccino. It's a perfect combination of sweetness and bitterness, the beans unburnt. It's probably some of the best coffee I've tasted in a long time.

The house itself is in an older part of town. It is a modest three bedroom. There are cars parked all over the place. A couple of the neighbors have them in their front yard. Infused with a jolt of caffeine, I open the newly painted white picket fence gate and knock, then press the doorbell. Unlike the neighbors, with some parts of the fence or siding worn and dilapidated, this house is definitely well cared for. There are flowers up front, the paint is fresh, and the windows are clean.

"Coming."

I hear a man's voice from inside. It takes him a

bit to get there, and when he opens the door, I can see why. Dressed in flannel pajamas, his hair is oily and sticking up in certain parts, unwashed, probably for days. His skin is sallow, so pale it's almost translucent, and his eyes are puffy like he has been crying.

"My name is Detective Kaitlyn Carr," I say, extending my hand. "Are you Steven Hilderbrand?"

He nods. I don't have any jurisdiction here, but I figured the title would give me a sense of gravitas and importance.

"You here about Cora?" he asks, taking a deep sigh.

"Yes. I have some questions to ask you."

"Sure. Come in."

The place is an odd combination of recently renovated, but also cluttered and disheveled. The couch is covered with three different throw blankets and a pillow from the bed where he had been sleeping. The coffee table is likewise almost invisible, covered in old takeout containers, a pizza box, napkins, beer bottles, and soda cans. There are a few Starbucks cups as well, laying around, emptied probably days ago.

"Sorry about the mess," he says without making a move to clean anything up. "It's been a rough time."

"Yes. I'm really sorry for your loss."

I take another look around and then he interrupts me and asks, "Why are you here exactly? I already told the other detectives everything."

"Actually, I'm not here on official business. I'm a detective with the LAPD, and I was just here on a trip. I was the one who found Cora on the trail."

"In the tree?" he asks, his mouth opening slightly, and I see how parched his lips are, cracked, almost bleeding.

"Yes, I was the one who found her body and made the report."

"Why are you here?"

"I wanted to talk to you about your relationship with her."

"Do I have to?"

"No, you don't have to. Her son Anthony came to see me, and he wants answers. He asked me for help."

"I guess," he says. "Sure."

He sits down on the edge of the couch, moving the throw blankets slightly out of the way, making an attempt to make room for me. I find a spot on the edge of the recliner.

"How do you know Cora?"

"We've been friends for a long time. Many years ago, I made the mistake of going out with her friend on a few dates. It didn't work out, but then Cora refused to date me, saying that it's girl code not to date your friend's exes. Our relationship became something more of a friendship after that. I got my hair cut at her salon. We spent time together. I helped her when she got pretty sick with MS and her son was at school, she didn't want him to know how sick he was.

"She could barely function, sometimes, had no energy whatsoever. I had to come around, help her out during the day, and give her enough energy to go and pick him up from school and take him to sports things. After that, she'd be drained."

"How did things become more romantic?"

"I owned an auto body repair shop. It was doing really well. Then I got an offer from Auto Boys, a nationwide chain. They made me an offer I couldn't resist. I didn't have a plan for retirement, really. Thought maybe I would sell the place. I didn't have kids. When this big pile of money came my way, I thought, "What if I were to just take it and move away somewhere warm? Somewhere where it's not raining so much. I told her the good news and she was so happy for me. Then she got sad and said that she'd really miss me. We talked about our relationship, and I told her that how I felt about her hadn't changed, that I love her, and if she doesn't want anything romantic with me, that's fine. She kissed me. That's when I found out that she had liked me for a long time, but she was worried about her friend and about getting into a relationship while her son was living with her. She didn't want to bring around anyone bad. She didn't want to be one of those moms that just hops from guy to guy. She had plenty of offers. Don't get me wrong. She was an incredible, beautiful woman who stayed in shape.

“She was so fun too, I told her that I didn't really have a reason to stay unless she gave me one. Then when we started seeing each other, we started to feel like maybe this could become something."

"What was the plan for the night that she disappeared?" I ask. He takes a deep breath. I can tell that he's holding back tears.

"She told her son that I was coming over, I knew him already. We'd met a number of times, and hung out together, but he knew me only as a friend. That night, we were going to tell him the truth, that we'd been seeing each other for a couple of months, and that it was serious."

"Was she nervous about it?"

"Yes, kind of, but more excited than anything. She just hated hiding anything from her son. They were so close and they were so good together. He is a good kid.

"I saw the pictures on social media," I say. "They were actually that close?"

"Probably even more so, there's a lot of stuff

that didn't get posted. They just had a lot of fun together. He had a troubled relationship with his father. Theodor had left her when Anthony was six months old. Actually, he didn't leave her. She found out that he was having an affair with her best friend. She kicked him out. He ended up moving in with her best friend and they ended up getting married. The whole situation was so crappy. Cora was traumatized. She was so hurt, but she wanted to make the best of it.

“Over the years, they were cordial. They had shared custody, and she never spoke bad about her ex-husband. Not even to me, she just stated the facts and said that she didn't want to bad-mouth him or vent about him or anything like that. She wanted Anthony to be close with his half-siblings and his stepmom, but they were just different people. His dad didn't get him coloring his hair. He didn't like that he played music. He thought that it made him a pansy. He wanted Anthony to play more sports."

"What were your plans that day?"

"Anthony was going to be there with his girlfriend, Evelyn. Cora liked her. We were just going to tell them that we were a couple now. She suspected that he knew something was up and she thought that he'd be happy for her because he’d been telling her to date someone for a long time, but she just didn't feel comfortable."

"Were you her first boyfriend in all those years?"

"Yes, pretty much. I never clicked with anyone before like this. I think that's what we had in common. It was good to be friends and get to know each other in this safe zone. Of course, I'd had a crush on her for a long time."

"What about her friend that you dated?"

"It was nothing, just fizzled out. We didn't have anything in common. We're still friendly. She knew as much as we did, that we didn't have much of a relationship."

I watch him tell the story and I listen to it. What I see is a broken man whose hopes of a wonderful relationship and a future have been dashed in a tragic and brutal manner. I ask him about what exactly happened that night. He tells me that he had dropped her off at work earlier in the morning after they went and got coffee together. She'd left her car at home, and he was going to pick her up after work. They were going to drive to her house and order dinner.

When he showed up at her studio, she wasn't there. He texted and called her a few times and then reached out to Anthony, he thought that she'd gotten a call for a last minute hairstyle and just didn't call him back.

"Did that happen often?" I ask.

"No, it happened once, but she called me

about it. It was this woman who had a hairstylist scheduled for her daughter's event and she canceled at the last minute. Cora called me then and told me that we just had to do it some other time. I wasn't sure what happened, but I tried not to worry. I thought maybe she had lost her phone or dropped it in the water and it wasn't working. She didn't have my number memorized. You try not to panic and just think that it's probably nothing because nothing like this ever happens, right? This is just like a bad dream or some television show or something."

"Yes, it's pretty terrible," I say.

"I just keep waiting to wake up," Steve says, "Just open my eyes and return to my normal life."

"What happened later that night?" I asked.

"Anthony called me. He said that his mom never showed up, asked me where she could be. He knew that we were going to come over that night. I told him that I'd had plans to pick her up, but she wasn't there, and the studio was closed. I wasn't sure what happened. I told him not to worry. I told him that it was probably nothing, that she probably went out on a call and maybe lost her phone, but he was frantic. Then his girlfriend's mom showed up and she was going to be there with him so I didn't go."

He begins to sob. He buries his head in his hands and his shoulders move up and down with each exhale. I put my arm around him and hold him tightly. There's nothing I can do to fix any of this. When he gets a hold of himself and wipes some of the tears, I ask him about the next 10 days.

"They were hell. For a while, the cops didn't take Anthony seriously. He called me and we looked for her. Then his father got involved and told him that he can't be missing school over this. He made a report and I corroborated it. I guess the police started looking at that point. This was a couple of days later, but they found nothing. We tried to get it on the news, but they said that 'There was no evidence that something had happened,' and there was a school shooting that was taking up all the bandwidth. That was what people were interested in, not a missing mom. This has been the longest 10 days and yet, I wish that I could go back and just be there in that space without knowing that she's gone, gone from this earth, never to be seen again. Our life was just about to begin. We had all of these plans."

"What plans?" I ask.

"We were going to wait until Anthony graduated and see where he went to school, but we were going to head south. He wanted to go to California. Maybe we'd go to Palm Springs or Arizona. I had money for a good retirement and she could always open another hair salon down there. I was going to stay here for another two years and then we were going to take off."

"You said Anthony didn't know anything about this?"

"She had told him a few times that maybe she'd come with him when he left. He seemed to be really into that idea. Not live with him, but live nearby. Like I said, they were super close."

"What about her ex-husband?"

"I don't know what he knew. He didn't want anyone looking for her. He didn't seem to care one bit that she was gone."

I bite my lower lip, "That's not a good sign. Did he seem surprised?"

"I don't know. Anthony never had anything good to say about him," Steven says. "She always stopped him from talking bad about his dad, with me there, but it was clear Anthony wasn't happy."

"And now he has to live with them full time," I say.

"How is he doing?"

"He's very distraught. He said that his dad wasn't interested in finding his mom. I guess that's one of the reasons why I'm here, why he reached out to me.

"You have to find out what happened because the police aren't working on it. You found her, maybe you can find the man who did this to her."

"I'll try," I say, "I'll do my best."

Chapter 18

I leave Steve Hildebrand's house with a profound sense of sorrow and loss. This man is wrecked, completely broken by what happened to the woman that he had fallen in love with. I could tell how much regret he has over not protecting her, showing up earlier, pressing the matter more. I wonder if he has any regrets about the fact that life just didn't work out for them earlier, that maybe if they had been together this whole time, it would have been different. I should head back to the hotel, talk to Luke and make some sort of plan about Donald, but this case wears on me.

The sadness runs deep. I'm just thankful that neither her son nor her boyfriend saw her up there in that tree like I did. That would be a terrible way to remember a loved one, and images like that get ingrained in your mind forever. I know because I saw my father's body in my parents' bedroom, surrounded by blood from the supposedly self-inflicted gunshot wound.

To this day, even though it has been years since that happened, I keep thinking about it. Whenever I think of him, that's the first image that pops in my head, not him teaching me to ride a bike, not him taking me skiing or kayaking on the lake, but that bloody, gory image of his legs laying limp beside him, his head scrunched into his neck, a shell of who he was as a person when he was alive, and all the blood everywhere. When you get shot in the stomach, you can bleed out for a very long time, you suffer. It could be hours before you actually pass away. When you finally do, you do so in pure agony. I hate that those were the last breaths that he took, in pain like that.

My heart goes out to Steve and Anthony because they have lost a loved one too. Her death should have never happened, but I would place all the money that I have in the world on a bet that it was not Steve who had done it.

I reach over to my phone and look up the directions to a new address. It takes me to a fancy, upscale neighborhood with tall, shiny new homes and expensive cars in the driveways. I parked my rental in front of the house and make a trek up the flagstone path laid into the manicured lawn. Here, a knock on the front door won't do, you have to ring the doorbell in order for people to hear you. The house is probably over 3,000 square feet, if not more.

A few moments later, someone comes downstairs. Melinda Rydell is a petite blonde with a big, bright smile and pearly white teeth. I introduce myself, and her face immediately falls.

"I'm so sorry that that happened," she says, avoiding using Cora's name.

"Is Theodor around? I really need to ask him a few questions." I had introduced myself as a Detective Kaitlyn Carr, but not clarified who I really was like I did with Steven. I figured there'd be time later in the conversation to point out my lack of jurisdiction.

"Yes. He's in the kitchen. Come on in."

I find Theodor behind the marble island, his head buried in his phone. It takes him a moment to look up at me after Melinda introduces me. He's in no rush to say hello, or shake my hand, or be helpful in any way. In fact, he's bordering on rudeness.

I double-check his story. He says that he was home that whole evening with Melinda and the kids until he got the frantic call from Anthony to pick him up.

"How's your relationship with Anthony?"

"As good as can be expected. Cora has always poisoned him against me."

This goes against everything that I have heard from not just Anthony himself, but Steven and even Captain Carville. So, I take that statement into consideration and make a mental note to remember it.

"Your relationship with Anthony is, what would you say, complicated?

"Distant," he says, and then turns his phone back on and starts to scroll through what looks to be his emails. "Listen, I don't really have time to talk about this again. I already gave my statement."

"Yes, I know, but I'm just double-checking a few things."

"I don't know why you don't talk to other people in the department. Why do you have to keep bothering me about this?"

This is my chance to say who I am, but I bite my tongue.

"Anthony tells me that he was concerned about his mom, but you don't seem to be?"

"I wasn't at that time. I guess he was right," Theodor says without looking away from his phone. "At that time, I wasn't particularly concerned. Anthony says she's reliable, but I've known her to be a bit flaky."

"What do you mean by that?"

"When he was little, she had a pill addiction. She was taking Xanax and some other antidepressants. It was getting a little bit out of hand. She actually had to go to rehab."

"What about after that?" I ask.

"She said she'd been sober for years, but how do you really know, right?"

"Wasn't she pretty reliable answering calls and making plans?"

"Yes, I guess so."

"Why weren't you worried about her when Anthony called?"

"Because Anthony is a little bitch," he says exasperated, slamming his phone down. "He exaggerates everything. Everything is a big deal. He has all these feelings to work out all the time. I'm sick of it. It's because she took him to therapy and got him talking about all these things that he should just ignore and they won't be a problem."

I swallow hard. Now I'm getting a true sense of what this guy is really like.

"Anthony wants to talk about this and that. Who has time for that, or the energy? They always acted like their relationship was so great, Anthony and Cora's, but in reality, look what happened. He didn't even know that she had a boyfriend. Who knows what else she was into?"

"What do you mean by that?" I ask. "Are you insinuating that she had a secret life?"

"Maybe. She was always pretty hot, and she says that she's making all that money at the studio, but cutting hair in Olympia, Washington, is it really that profitable?"

"What are you trying to say, sir?"

"You know what I'm trying to say. She's a pretty girl. You meet a guy for a few dates. He pays you $300, $500 a pop up in Seattle at their inflated prices, and then you say that you made all that in tips cutting hair."

"I've never heard that from anyone before. Have you made that statement to other people?"

"No, but you're here coming around asking me questions. You're trying to make me speculate, right?"

"No, that's the last thing I want you to do. I don't want you to speculate. I want you to tell me your experience of what the truth was, of what really happened."

"What really happened was that Anthony called me, upset that his mom hadn't come back from work. I picked him up. I took him home. He's been here ever since. For ten days, none of us knew what was wrong or what had happened. He was completely lost, freaking out, crying. Nothing would make him calm down. Then the cops came and told us that they found her dead body up some tree, tied up there like a scarecrow. How the hell does that happen? That's all I know. She was my ex-wife. What else do you want me to say?"

I walk out at a loss as to where to go from

here. There was something very unpleasant about Theodor in his attitude about everything, but could he also be telling the truth? Was she an escort? Of course, none of that would justify what had happened to her, but is there a direction that the cops should look at that involved that line of work? I try to think about how you'd find out whether someone was really an escort.

Phones and laptops, digital fingerprints. Unless she had a secret phone that she used to communicate with people. At this point, I don't even know if she was an escort at all, if she was involved with anything like that, but I know that I have to talk to Captain Carville and try to get to the bottom of this before things get even more complicated.

Chapter 19

Later that evening, I get a call from Captain Carville asking me to pop by the station again when I have time. I decide to stop by before grabbing some dinner and I feel like we are in this limbo. How many days do we stay in the area? Depends entirely on my decision as to how much I'm willing to help Donald, but I've yet to make that decision. I've just talked to Steve and Theodor earlier in the day, but I haven't told the captain or Detective Mitchell about what Theodor told me about her being an escort.

The thing is that, as a witness, I wasn't supposed to talk to either one of them or go around acting as if I have any investigative power whatsoever. I wasn't officially hired as a private investigator by Anthony. This is all just a favor and talking to his father wasn't even something he had asked me to do.

"Who do you think you are?" Captain Carville comes right at me as soon as he sees me.

I was thinking of taking my time and easing into this conversation, but I realize that I've been found out.

"You have no right to talk to possible suspects in this case. Why did you go over there like you work for our department? You are not a detective up here. I could have you cited for impersonating an officer."

"I did no such thing."

"Did you ever tell Theodor, Anthony's father, that you were the one that found her body?"

I look down at the floor.

"Did you ever tell him that you're not working the case? Or did you come forward and introduce yourself as Detective Kaitlyn Carr?"

"Look, I was going to tell him everything, but I wanted to ask him some questions first."

"You have no right. This isn't your case. This doesn't involve you in any shape or form."

"It does involve me. I found the body, and Anthony came to talk to me. He asked me for my help."

"I don't care about that. Did he hire you as a private investigator?"

"No, he didn't."

"Then you had no right talking to her boyfriend or her ex-husband about any of this."

"Listen, I was just trying to be helpful."

"No, you were being nosy. You found the body and that wasn't good enough. You thought you'd help out in some other way."

"Look," I say putting my hand up to stop him from going on and on.

"Don't you put your hand up in the air in front of me," he says. "I'm a captain."

"You're not my captain," I snap, "I don't work for you."

"Exactly. You're a witness. How do I even know that you're telling me the truth? Maybe you had something to do with this murder," he says holding his arms across his chest. "Maybe you would like to spend a night in jail for not telling me the truth. If you want to fight that and hire a lawyer and try to get back at me, well then go right ahead."

"You would arrest me even though you know that I have nothing to do with this?"

"I don't like people messing with my case. I will do what is necessary to make sure you keep your nose out of it."

"Theodor told me something that I'm not sure that he told Detective Mitchell or anyone else."

He tilts his head and stares at me waiting for me to continue.

"He suspected that Cora was an escort. I don't know if this is the truth or if this is just him talking in a bad way about his ex-wife. He also told me a lot of things about her that didn't seem to be true."

"Like what?"

"Like she was poisoning Anthony against him. He was blaming her for them having a rift, but from everything that you and Detective Mitchell told me, that wasn't the case."

I wait for him to say something, but he doesn't, instead, there's a long pause. For a moment I glance down at his desk, the top of which had not seen sunlight in a long time as it's covered in paperwork and folders.

"He mentioned she might be an escort, but in that way where he didn't seem to be sure where her money was coming from. He didn't think it was all coming from styling hair. Now, he could be mad about her boyfriend, just about the divorce still, I don't know, but I came here to tell you this."

"No, I don't think so. I don't think you were going to admit talking to him."

"Yes, I was," I say. "Of course, I was. There are certain things you should know about the case and that was one of them. Now, I don't know how true it is, but I was going to ask you to check her phone and her computer, any other digital devices she had for any evidence of her meeting with men, if that's indeed something that might have happened."

He exhales loudly and then heads over to his desk and takes a few long gulps of his Coke. It's in a tall plastic cup and I can hear the ice rattling around as he sucks on the straw.

"I don't like my witnesses talking to suspects," he says.

"Are either of them suspects really, between you and me?"

"Theodor is," Captain Carville admits.

"I got that sense as well," I nod. "He was very detached and cold and barely looked up from his phone when he talked to me. I'm going to go now," I say after another long pause when the awkwardness gets to be unbearable.

He catches me by the doorway and says, "Maybe I got a little bit heated there, but I don't like anyone going around impersonating being an officer working for my precinct."

"I understand that and I'm sorry. That was honestly not my attention. I was going to come right out and tell him the truth."

"Fine. I'll check out the escort angle, see if there's anything to it."

I give him a nod. "Will you keep me in the loop as to what you find?" I add.

"Maybe."

That's good. I'll take a maybe, I decide and

walk out feeling sick to my stomach like I had just eaten something rancid.

I haven't had a dressing down like that since I was in the academy, but I admit to myself that it was wrong to pretend to be a detective working this case when in reality I'm anything but. When I get back to Luke, I suggest that we pay Boyden Paper Company a visit.

Chapter 20

My drive to North Portland, Oregon is not planned by any stretch of the imagination. It's a little bit over two hours south of Olympia. On the drive down, Luke keeps asking me what I expect to find.

"He's just some guy who works for a printing shop. So, you follow him from work to his house and then what? Stakeouts take a long time, days and days of work to get anything. One trip out to see him isn't going to change anything."

Luke isn't saying anything that I don't already know. I've been on multiple stakeouts. They're tedious and boring work. You sit in your car, you wait until someone comes out, but you can't look down, you can't play on your phone or watch anything on your iPad. At least in an ideal situation. You just sit, watch, and wait, maybe have a snack here or there, or a cup of coffee.

"I've been to one where I was there for twenty days," I say. "Those were probably the longest days of my life."

"What about now? What are you looking for?"

"I don't know. I guess I just want to see him."

"What if he doesn't look like a serial killer?" Luke jokes.

"I just wish I hadn't had that fight with Donald. I wish I'd let him open up to me more and show me his files. Maybe then I wouldn't be in this situation."

"And yet you're going over there," Luke says. "What are you trying to find out?"

He's asking me questions that I have no answer to.

We drive past a lumber yard, an abandoned railroad. The pines start to tower around us, and the road gets narrower and full of trees in foliage. I want to drive out to the coast to see the water and the ocean, but it's surprisingly far away, except for out where the Columbia River intersects between Washington and Oregon, just a little bit north of Portland. Near massive states like California and Montana, it is easy to forget that Washington is larger than any state east of the Mississippi River. Outside of the few population centers, though, it is sparsely inhabited, with only a few winding highways snaking out to the vast, wet wilderness of the Olympic Peninsula.

Luke is at the wheel until we go through a Starbucks drive-through and I get us the rest of the way. Unfortunately, we won't be able to make it all the way to Portland and visit Powell's, their famous bookstore, we're here to do a job.

I know the location of the Boyden Paper company. I remember that Donald had mentioned that he was no longer working on the road as much. Chances are he'll be there.

"Do you remember what he looks like?" Luke asks, sucking down his green matcha iced tea latte, which I had tried once. It tasted too much like soap for my liking.

The paper company is a nondescript office building with a parking lot out front and an entrance straight from the street. There are a number of other businesses in the office park, but nothing flashy or fancy. No retail stores or restaurants. Just a notary public, a CPA, and an air conditioning repair company listed on the sign out front.

The dreariness and the lack of sunlight of the last couple of days are finally starting to get to me. I'm no longer appreciating the greenness of the trees and the foliage, but, in fact, yearning to go back to a place where the sky is high and the clouds are almost non-existent.

Luckily, the office park is visible from the street, and I don't have to go inside the parking lot to see the front. We wait and within half an hour, the day becomes interminable.

"You know what he looks like?" Luke asks and I realized that he hadn't even seen the picture of him that I saw briefly in the manila folder.

"I saw a glimpse. Average build, brown hair, brown eyes. 60s, maybe 50s. White, a flatter face and wider nose, but no other identifying characteristics really."

"So, a white guy with brown hair, that's who we're looking for?" Luke jokes.

"You didn't have to come. I told you where I was headed."

"Hey, spending some time in a car with you just talking, I don't have a problem with that. I'm just trying to warn you that you may not be able to find what you think you're looking for here."

I give him a shrug. He's right. Of course, he's right. He's an FBI agent with a lot of years of experience and we have no real business being here except that I just want to get a look at this alleged connection to my father's death.

"I know for certain," I say, "that if I were to see him again, I'd be able to identify him as the guy that I saw in the picture."

"Okay, so say that you do. What happens when you follow him home," he asks, "and you discover that he lives in an apartment down some road with equally average-looking houses? What is it going to tell you? Say he says hi to his neighbor, waves hello? Is he lying or is he just a friendly guy? Say he doesn't say hi, just drives right into his garage, what could that possibly mean?"

"What are you trying to say?" I unbuckle my seatbelt and I turn to face him, propping my arm up on the steering wheel.

"What I'm trying to say is that you're reading tea leaves here. You're going to make inferences and assumptions about who this guy is based on what you see. That's not great police work."

"I'm just trying to get a feeling for *who* he is."

"By looking at where he works and how he drives his car to his house? I've watched someone for thirty-five days once. He just went from home to work, or to the grocery store and back. It told me nothing about who he is, really. It's not like we're tapping his phone or seeing his text messages or his emails, that's at least some information."

I can't help but agree. Of course, he's right. I know that.

"Look, I don't really have any other option. I'm trying to decide if I want to help Donald or not. I know that he lied to be about my father or at least obfuscated the truth, but then he came out and told me what he knows. I want to see what is really there and, I don't know, I guess I just want to see if he's a nut or not."

"Again, not sure that following this guy is going to tell you one thing or another. You have to look at the actual case files."

"I know, but I blew up at him, and—" I pause, trying to collect my thoughts. "Look, if you're just going to complain like this, you can get out. I can drive around, try to find a bookstore or coffee shop for you to go to. I'd suggest a hike, but it's so freaking wet out."

He smiles.

"No, I'll stay here and annoy you. I don't mind."

"Thanks," I say sarcastically. "I really appreciate that."

Another hour passes watching paint dry. I break the cardinal rules of a good stakeout officer and check my phone. At first, there're just a few messages here and there, but then I read whole articles without even bothering to look up. The truth is that I don't even know if he's at work today.

I consider going inside, maybe asking to speak to him. Would that be so wrong? If he's there, maybe I could pretend to be someone else, but then my cover will be blown. I'd have to ask him specific questions and have a real reason to be here. Otherwise, he'd remember me, and if he were to ever see me again, he'd know that it has nothing to do with what I talked to him about.

I try to force myself to close the news app and stop doom scrolling through social media, but it's hard to explain just how boring it is to stare at a building all day. All the doubts you start to have about whether or not this person is even there today. I suddenly wonder if it's even a work day. Did I choose a weekend to come? No, I haven't. I am, however, wasting my precious vacation on this stupidity and that starts to make me feel angry as well.

Then just like that, the door swings open. A man in a suit comes out. There have been others that have come out the main entrance. Each one, I had carefully looked at with the telephoto lens on the camera that I brought to take pictures of whales, of all things, and they weren't him, but this guy?

"I think that's him," I whisper under my breath. I take a picture and show it to Luke.

"I have no idea what he looks like," he says. I roll my eyes. He's still trying to mess with me. I watch as the man walks towards us straight at me, not looking down on his phone, just straight ahead, carrying a briefcase. I know it's him, the way that you just recognize someone that you know.

"That's him. I'm certain that's him." I say.

"What do you want to do now?"

"That I'm not so certain about." I shrug. I watch as he walks over to his gray Saab, gets in and starts the engine. He pulls out quickly, carefully looking around and then drives out of the parking lot towards us and to the left.

"Follow behind him, but not too close." Luke says. I nod. I know the address of his house, another thing that I saw on the file, and when Luke types it into his Google Maps, I see that he's not headed there at all. In fact, he gets onto the highway and starts driving west.

"Where is he going?" I ask. I stay two cars behind him, but I'm grasping onto the steering wheel so tightly, my knuckles are turning white. I'm nervous and uncertain and anxious all at once.

"He's probably just going to Costco or running some errands," I say to Luke.

"Stores are all back in town," he says under his breath.

"Maybe he's meeting up with someone."

He shrugs.

"That's definitely a possibility, but who and why?"

The fact that I would catch him doing something illicit or at all compromising the first time that I watch him is beyond unlikely. I know that I probably have a greater likelihood of getting picked up by an alien and beamed up to space. That kind of stuff just doesn't happen, but I'm curious. I know that we're not headed to his house and that we're headed away from most big box stores. So, *where* are we going?

Chapter 21

We drive west for about forty-five minutes. A couple of times I feel like I might lose him. There are a number of gray Saabs around, but Luke helps me, points me to the right one. We're headed deeper into the woods where the trees surround both sides of the road and there are not so many strip malls on each side. Darkness slowly starts to fall. I turn toward Luke and ask where we're going multiple times. He follows the map on his phone as we try to figure out if there is any point to any of this.

"What if he's just driving around?" I finally say. "Clearing his head or something like that."

"People usually do that in a small radius, or at least I know that's what I do for myself," Luke says. "And you."

"Yes. If I were to take a drive, it'd be like

twenty or thirty minutes, maybe. One direction, no more. This seems like he's going somewhere specific, though."

It sounds like he turns on his blinker and then veers to the right. I follow behind him, but the cars in between us continue on straight. I keep going until all the other cars disappear.

"Do you think he's going to spot me?" I ask.

"He doesn't know who you are."

"True. It's hard to see faces through the rear window of a car looking through someone's windshield."

Luckily, the Honda we had rented is pretty generic.

"Where do you think he's headed?" I ask again.

"I don't know."

He makes another left and then a right. He pulls into a small residential neighborhood and out in the distance I see an elementary school. There's a fence all around, but he pulls into the parking lot. I follow him.

"What is he doing here? Does he have any kids?" Luke asks.

I shrug. "Not little ones. They're all grown."

He looks up the time. It's around pickup time, 3:30.

"I guess he's just running an errand after all, right?" I ask, hoping for the best. I follow behind him and park in the parking lot, but about twenty cars behind. I wait for him to get out and head in to pick someone up, but he doesn't. He just sits in his car as close to the entrance as possible, but doesn't move.

Luke and I exchange looks. He's waiting for someone. Moms come and go. A few dads show up. Everyone parks their cars and gets out as quickly as possible. There's no waiting around.

Nobody else just sits in their car. The only woman that does show up a little early and then sit in the front seat is texting furiously on her phone. Then as soon as someone else pulls up next to her, she waves hello to her friend, and they walk together to get their kids. This is a preschool along with an elementary school. The majority of kids that come out are ages three to six. Every time I glance over at David Trincia, he's still there.

"I'm going to walk out," Luke says.

"What about me?"

"If he spots you and then he sees you again, he'll probably remember you more. You're too pretty," he says and I roll my eyes with a smile.

"What's your plan?"

He gives me a shrug and slams the door shut. He heads up towards the school like he's going to pick up a kid.

Is he actually going to ring the doorbell? I wonder to myself, but he doesn't.

I watch as Luke walks over to the door. He then grabs his phone. He looks down, typing seriously. If you weren't looking, you wouldn't know that he was actually looking at the silver Saab. He then brings the phone to his ear, wanders back and forth, moving his mouth, and I wonder if he's actually talking to someone. A minute later, a woman in her 30s gets out of a car to pick up her child, and my phone rings.

"Hey, it's me. Just need to have someone to actually talk to, since, you know, somebody's walking over to me."

I laugh. "What do you see?"

"He's sitting in his car," he says, walking around and gesturing wildly, as if he is frustrated with someone on the other end.

"You know, it's really weird to see you talk like that to someone who's clearly not there. You're quite a good liar."

"I prefer actor," Luke whispers and continues to gesture. "He's just sitting there," he says. "He's got a phone, and he looks like he's taking pictures, but that's it."

"Of what?"

"You can't see it from the parking lot, but from here you can see the kids are in the back playing. There's a large fence," he says, walking further away from the woman who is about to pick up her kids. He takes a few steps away.

"Keep talking to me," he says. "I need to look like I'm busy."

I start to say something, but he just storms off.

"Okay, I'm coming back now. Fine," he says, nods hello to one of the other parents and then continues toward me in a frustrated, annoyed manner before getting into the car.

"What happened?"

"Nothing. Just figured I couldn't stay out there too long without drawing his suspicion. He's definitely taking pictures of the kids."

"Why?"

"I don't know," he says.

"Like you think he's going to take one?" I ask.

"I have no idea. Who are some of the victims that Donald suspects he murdered?" He asks.

"One of them is a child, but the others, I believe, are adults."

"You didn't talk to him about it?"

"I did, but I was trying to-- The type of victim didn't match up, like they weren't all single women, prostitutes, that kind of thing."

"Maybe there's a good reason that he would be sitting here."

"And that is?"

"Maybe he's picking up his grandchild. Maybe there's some sort of custody battle between his child and the ex-partner and he's trying to track what time they're getting picked up if they're intoxicated or whatever. I don't know."

I nod my head. "Yes, I guess that's a possibility. But I don't think he has kids. What do we do now? Do we just leave him here watching these kids?"

Half an hour later, fifteen minutes after we get there when most of the kids are picked up, the gray Saab pulls out of the parking lot and drives away. I follow him back onto the highway, back to Portland, where he pulls into his own driveway, gets out of the car, and goes inside a bluish house with gray shingles.

It's a craftsman that hasn't been remodeled much. It's in an okay neighborhood. Nothing spectacular, but not too shabby, either. There are no cars parked on the front lawn, but there's not one luxury vehicle in sight. The lots are small and modest, and there are American flags waving proudly in the wind.

"What now?" I ask. He shrugs.

"I'm assuming that whatever child he was watching is safe for now." I

I want to notify the school. Notify them of what, exactly? From the outside, it looks safe. The parents have to press a button to be let in, have to sign out with their child. There are some kids playing in the backyard behind the gate, but they're not exactly visible from the street. The school seems to be taking as many precautions as necessary. If I were to call them, what would I say exactly? A guy that some retired FBI agent suspects of being a serial killer, with absolutely no proof, drove here from work and sat in your parking lot for 15 minutes, took some pictures, and drove off.

"What if I were to call them?" I say to Luke. "Then they can be on alert for his car."

"Yes. I guess it's worth a shot."

"I just want to do everything in my power to protect those kids. I have no idea what his intentions are," I say, looking up the name and number of the school on Google. As soon as the secretary answers, I ask for the principal. I introduce myself, give her some broad information, scare her sufficiently, but also promise that I do not have proof of anything. This could be completely innocent. She sounds shaken. It's the end of the day and a call like this would disturb anybody.

The principal listens and sighs.

"Let's say it is nothing," the principal says after a long pause, her voice uncertain all of a sudden, unlike the woman who had answered the phone earlier. "What could it mean? Why was he doing that?"

"The thing is, that I have no idea."

"He may have a grandchild in the school, but photographs make no sense."

"Maybe there is a custody battle for a friend of his or his own child."

"I'm not certain that he has any kids," I say.

"You're not exactly putting me at ease."

"I'm not making this call to put you at ease, ma'am. If you see him again, please give me a call." I give her the license plate and I tell her exactly what building he was parked in front of.

"One of your teachers at the other building should be able to spot his car without leaving the premises. If he comes back, it will probably be around pick up time again. Just let me know, okay?"

Chapter 22

I make plans to meet up with Anthony at the coffee shop, and even though I arrive on time, he's there already, nervously looking out the window, tapping his fingers on the Formica table. His hair is bright purple now, the curls falling over his face masking some of the bad acne around the T-zone and the cheeks. When I give him a hug, I can feel him shaking.

"How are you doing?" I ask as I take him up to the counter with me to order him something to drink. He surprises me by getting a tall black espresso, no cream or sugar, an unlikely choice for a teenager. He says that he's been drinking that for a couple of years now.

"It was Mom's favorite drink too," he says, swallowing hard and fighting back tears. "Even though she liked her lattes and the bright pink dragon fruit one as well."

I give him a knowing smile and get my iced tea. It's drizzling outside. The day has been gray since the morning, and I find myself pining for the bright blue skies of Southern California. I also get a brownie, thick, moist, and big enough to share, but he doesn't take a bite.

"How's everything with your dad?"

"Terrible," Anthony says. "I hate living with him. He doesn't understand, he doesn't think any of this is a big deal."

"What does he think happened to your mom?"

"He has no idea, but he seems to think that she's had all these boyfriends, guys that she's been out with, and she hasn't."

I tilt my head, wondering how much he knows. His father had suggested that she might have been an escort, but we found no proof of that whatsoever. Of course, it doesn't mean that it's not true, but putting that on Anthony right now feels cruel. Instead, I try to think of questions to ask him to try to elicit some more information. We talk a little bit about what it was like to have her as a mother, and he tells me how caring and loving she always was.

"It was just the two of us," Anthony says, "for years and years, and I liked it that way, but when I got a little bit older, I realized that it's not normal. She had to have her own personal life. Maybe a romance or something. I mean, that's what I wanted, and that's what I wanted for her as well."

"Were you pushing her to date?"

"Yes, kind of. Just making jokes here and there."

"Did you ever get the sense that she was in fact dating and maybe didn't want to tell you?"

"Yes." He nods. "A little bit. I figured that she might have been seeing someone."

"If you were such close friends, why wouldn't she tell you about it?"

"Because she never crossed the line. I could always come to her about anything, and she would listen and comfort me. She would talk to my teachers if I were having trouble or the parents of the other kid who was being mean. She always tried to make things better, but she never put her crap on me. She wasn't one of those moms that would confide in me about her personal life and make me worry. You know what I mean? The ones who talk too much. She wasn't like that at all."

"What are you trying to say exactly?" I asked.

"Well, she never told me about age-inappropriate things. She talked a little bit about money, but I didn't know much about it. She didn't want me to worry about things that I couldn't deal with.

That's what you're supposed to do as a parent, right?"

I nod. This kid knows more about parenting than most of the people that I encounter at work, and for a moment there, I find that both shocking and a relief when thinking about the future. Maybe cycles of abuse can be broken. Maybe you can come out of poverty, move past parents who don't know much about how to parent. You can get out of it, and you can be a good mom.

"What about your father?" I ask.

"My father expects me to be one way. He wants me to be good at sports. He hates the fact that my hair is pink, well, purple now, and I have pimples on my face. He wants me to be this jock. He wants me to be mean to the scrawny kids who wear glasses and play video games. I'm just not like that. My mom raised me better than that and so he doesn't get it. He doesn't understand anything about me. One of the reasons I dye my hair is that my mom showed me how to do it. We had talked about me making it purple for a little bit. This is a memory of her for the funeral.

She was always supportive of me expressing myself as who I really am and just trying on different looks, different ways of being. She was there for me in ways that no one else was and now she's gone, and I'm stuck with him."

"Look, I know that you have problems with

your father right now," I say, interjecting. "But I'm sure he loves you."

"No, he doesn't." Anthony shakes his head. "He loves his other family. He maybe likes the idea of me, but he doesn't like the reality. He wants to control me with money. He wants me to work for him and he wants me to look right and act right and be his little puppet. I'm just not into that, and I'm never going to be, because I know what happens to people like that. When they're fifty, they still have to ask permission to paint their houses because the house was originally owned by their parents. I'm not going to be like that. I'm going to make my own money. I'm not going to answer to anyone, least of all him."

I listen to the depth of insight with which he speaks, and I'm surprised at how much he seems to understand about the world that so few adults do.

"I can't tell you what to do or how to feel, you know that, right?"

"Yes. I don't want you to, I just want you to find my mom's killer."

"That's the one thing that I can try. I'm going to try my best. But you have to be absolutely honest with me, Anthony."

"About what?"

"I didn't want to bring this up, but you know

her so well that you really are the only person I can ask."

"What?" he asks. "What are you talking about?"

"Well, is there any chance that your mother had another way to make an income?"

"What are you talking about?" He sits back, finishing the last of his coffee and putting the cup carefully back on the table .

"I know that she had the salon and it did pretty well, but she was a beautiful woman who you said never dated, but is there any chance that she had a reason to meet men? Like maybe--"

He looks at me blankly. I'm trying to be careful with my words to not be offensive in any way, but I am still talking to a teenager who's not really reading between the lines.

"Would she have any reason to meet with a lot of men? Is there any way that she could have--"

He looks at me and blinks.

"Is there any way that she could have met with men for companionship or anything else like that?"

He stares at me again. I'm going to have to be even more clear.

"We got wind that she might have been an escort, perhaps." I finally say, going with the less offensive word escort rather than prostitute.

"No, absolutely not," he says.

"I don't want you to get offended. There's nothing wrong with being a sex worker," I say. "That doesn't say anything about your mother. I'm just trying to find out all the people that she has been in contact with, and those would be the people that I would then look at. This isn't an indictment of her character in any way."

"Look, I don't have any issues with sex work. People do what they have to for work, to make a living. There are many that don't do it because there are abused or on drugs or all of those other stereotypes. I know all that. My mom was very sex-positive, but she was always home in the evenings. When I did clubs and sports on week-ends and I had games, she was there, and during the day she was at work so I don't know when she would have had time to meet up with these men, but it wasn't when I saw her after school or on weekends. She was home."

I give him a nod. This I believe. I decide for myself that I'll have to talk to people at her salon to find out if she left at any point or at least on any consistent basis, but I reach out to him for one more thing.

"Do you know her login information to her iCloud?"

"Yes," he says. "In fact, I can log in from my laptop right here."

He pulls it out of his backpack, puts it on the

table and we go through her emails and through all her files on the desktop. Nothing. No phone numbers, no secret files. It's all blank.

"Is there any possibility that she could have had another phone?" I ask.

"I guess, but I never saw one. I know what you're trying to do. You're trying to make her like a spy, someone with this whole other life, but I spent so much time with her. It was just the two of us. I would have known if she was lying."

"What about her relationship? This new boyfriend. You knew nothing about that."

"I knew that she was meeting up with him," Anthony says. "I mean, I knew they were spending time together as friends, and I suspected that something was up, and I was just giving her time to think about it."

"Is there any chance that he could have had something to do with this?"

Anthony looks up at me.

"I don't know. I mean, I guess anything is possible, but I didn't think so at the time."

His lip starts to quiver, and he can't hold back the tears. They suddenly overwhelm him, and the grown-up put-together young adult melts before me into a puddle of loss and sadness.

Chapter 23

I watch Anthony drive away before returning to the coffee shop to use the bathroom. As soon as I exit, Donald shows up, dressed in a suit and tie like he's going to work. He gets up from one of the chairs, coffee in hand, and approaches me.

"This isn't an accident, is it?" I say.

"This is a small town, but I followed you here. I admit it."

The blue suit is a little bit tight at the buttons, and I wonder if this is the suit that he had worn to work before he retired, or before he was forced into retirement. Now, it is one of the only ones that still fits. He plays with the buttons nervously, a small thing in his otherwise calm demeanor that betrays how he's feeling inside.

"What about the coffee?"

"Well, when I saw you come back in to use the

bathroom, I figured, why not? I should at least patronize the place."

"Were you here the whole time?"

"No, outside waiting. Didn't want to interfere with your investigation. That was the boy? The boy with the purple hair."

"It was his mother who was killed."

"Any leads?"

"Boyfriend, husband. The usual suspects."

He gives me a knowing nod.

"Boyfriend seems to be on the up and up, has an alibi, very upset."

"What about the husband?"

"It's an ex many, many years ago, so the motive isn't exactly there. Why would he do it after all this time? He's remarried. She's not. He has a whole other family. She's just taking care of their son. Not a lot of things make sense about this case.

"Did he have contact with her recently?"

"No. He claimed that she was moonlighting as an escort, but there seems to be no proof of that, whatsoever. I keep looking in case there's another phone or something else, but it's like she's a spy. No trail, digital or otherwise. Her salon was making good money. Her son says that she was with him all nights, evenings, weekends. Not exactly sure how much escorts would make for ten a.m. dates, but I have to rule out everything."

"You told the son?"

"Yes, in not so many words. He showed me her iCloud account for emails. Nothing. Unless there's a burner phone and a whole other identity. That's going to be a hard one to prove."

"The ex-husband making that up, what would be the reason?"

"I'm not sure. They divorced when that teenager you saw was a little kid, so at least a decade, if not more. Didn't have a great relationship but started to become civil more recently."

"What about custody?"

"He's 15. It's really up to him at this point if he wants to spend time with his dad, but dad doesn't seem to be so into spending time with him, however."

"Oh, really?"

"Well, he made it seem like he wants him to be a tough guy, football player, basketball player, popular. From the way he looks, he might be a popular musician in about 10 years, but definitely not one for competitive sports."

"I don't know. I guess alibis, you got to check exactly where they were, what they did."

"That's the hard part," I say, "I'm not exactly on this case. He just reached out to me wanting my help because he thinks the police aren't doing enough. They didn't even want to take his statement initially when she went missing."

"That's a tough one."

I give him a slight nod.

"I get the sense that you're not here to talk about my semi-formal private investigation."

"No, not at all. I need your help, Kaitlyn. I need you to go to talk to this guy in prison."

"I'm still mad at you," I say, crossing my arms and continue to stand outside of the bathroom. He waves to me to take a seat next to him on the burnt orange velvet couch. Reluctantly, I agree.

"There are three murders here. One of them is a child, preschool age. If this guy has anything to do with it, if this is a lead, he's the only one who would know."

I tilt my head, narrow my eyes, "Why me?"

"I burned a lot of goodwill. People don't believe me."

"I can see why."

"Look, I'm sorry. I wasn't as forthcoming about everything, but I just want you to go talk to him. Whatever you say goes. You talk to him, and you say that he's full of crap. That's the end."

"Really?" I arch my eyebrow.

"No," Donald reaches over and puts his hand on my forearm. "I'm telling you the truth. You don't think I know that it sounds like I'm losing my mind? Of course, I do. I'm just not sure I could believe anymore. Everything inside of me tells me that this is true, that this guy is telling me what he knows about his uncle, and this is a lead, but hey, maybe everyone else is right. Maybe I'm just a fool. I've decided that if you go and talk to him, and you tell me that you don't get the sense that what he's saying is true, then that's it. I'm done."

I furrow my brow and position myself at the edge of the seat, I don't quite believe him. This is probably just another tactic, but he leans over, looks me straight in the eye, and pleads, "I need a sounding board. My wife listens, but she's not in law enforcement. I've burned a lot of bridges and I can't trust anyone local. I don't know who else can help me, except for you."

"The fact that you're skeptical is good," Donald says, "But I don't want it to cloud your judgment. I just want you to go to the prison with me. I put your name on the list just in case, because it just takes so long to get approval. I just want you to come with me and let me know if any of this makes any sense. His story is compelling, at least I think so," but if it's not, if you don't believe it, then that will be it, I'll let it go."

"I don't think you will," I say, "Let's be honest, let's say I go along with this and I meet with him, if I don't believe him, you're not going to drop it. I'm just going to be one of the naysayers."

He looks hurt by this.

"You're different."

"Why?"

"Because I knew your father, and because you'd be the only person to ever talk to this guy, to my informant, everyone else just looked at the paperwork, but it's not just his story. It's how he tells it. There are three murders at stake. Three lives, three people with families who have no answers as to what happened: a little boy, the teenage runaway and the young woman. They deserve justice. They deserve for someone to find the truth. This guy who killed them, this wasn't his first time. It's probably not his last. You know as well as I do that he'll keep doing this until we stop him."

"How soon would you need me to go to the prison?" I asked. "Now, I'm not agreeing to anything. I'm just asking a question here."

"I understand. Monday is the soonest. You've been approved."

"I can't believe that you put my name on the list and signed all that paperwork."

"I didn't forge anything. I just put your name on the list so that it would run through the databases and make sure that you have no criminal record."

"I'm sure it all got streamlined once they found out that I work in law enforcement.

"Yes, that did speed things up a bit," he smiles.

I'm about to say that I'll think about it. The thing is that I don't really want to. I want to just make a decision here and now and live with it, whatever it is. He waits for me with anticipation. I can't help but frown. I bite my lower lip and the inside of my cheek. I'm not sure if I can give him the answer that he wants and then with a deep sigh, I say, "Fine." I say, “Maybe."

Chapter 24

The prison has a distinctive smell of bleach and hard chemicals splattered all over linoleum floor and then cleaned up. It was as if someone were trying to desperately convince the visitors that this place was adequately cleaned when it was probably anything but that. Donald was right, the approval process to get me through was a breeze. He had put me on the list, and I didn't have to wait long. This was a minimum security prison after all with much fewer restrictions.

I've only been to jail as part of my duty as a patrol officer occasionally working in the courts, but I was pleasantly surprised when I didn't see any glass separation and prisoners sitting around tables with their family members, with permission to touch and feel and embrace. It was particularly helpful in cases when there were little kids, four or five-year-olds who couldn't understand why they couldn't see their dads.

Since Donald and I were not family members, he couldn't come with me. Though at first, I felt a little bit nervous about that, I realized that it would be a lot easier this way to get to the bottom of all of this. I'm here to find out if Victor is telling the truth, and if Donald was here influencing him in any way, that would interfere with the investigation.

I sit down at the far table near the vending machine and wait for him to come out. After five minutes of twiddling my thumbs because I couldn't bring in my phone, a guard brings him to the door. He's a pretty average-looking middle-aged man with a bit of a receding hairline, but nothing too tragic. He looks rested and relatively fit, but from the pictures that Donald had shown me, I knew that he used to be quite heavy. Within a few minutes of talking to me, he mentions that he has lost over 30 pounds and he is glad that he has so much time on his hands to exercise.

He has a friendly and direct manner. He looks me straight in the eye, not shy about smiling, hiding almost nothing about who he really is. He reminds me of the best kind of salesman, the ones that know when to leave you alone in the store and know when to approach when you have a question, but not a minute before that. We chit-chat about nothing in particular at first. This is something I've learned in my experience as a detective. If you want to get someone talking and to open up to you, they have to trust you. You can't come at them with hard-hitting questions. It's all about making friends, building a rapport.

He asked me about working for the LAPD and even shares that he had thought about wanting to be a detective. He had always wanted to be a detective as a kid but got sidetracked and chose a different way to make money instead when he got to be of age.

"I've always admired what you do, finding bad guys, that kind of thing. That's what connected me with Donald in the first place."

"Even if you are, technically, one of the bad guys?" I asked, allowing him to lead the conversation for the time being.

"Yes, of course." He shrugs, "Mysteries and thrillers have always been my favorite go-to book, and I've read so many good ones now that I have time in prison."

"You seem to be enjoying yourself here?" I say.

He leans back, tilts his head, and laughs. "I'm the kind of person who always tries to make the best of things. You don't know this about me, but there was a time when I fought against everything and everybody. Someone told me to go left and I went right. I was just that kind of personality, contrary to everything, and then I got arrested, just a DUI, not a huge deal. I just went on the straight and narrow."

I look at his hands. They are folded carefully in front of me casually without an inkling of nervousness or anxiety.

"So, what changed?" I ask.

"I kind of hit rock bottom then. I was 24. I knew I was headed for jail, more problems, was drinking too much so I just quit. I went super straight edge. Didn't fight anymore. Decided to go the other way. That's when I got into all the cop shows and the detective novels. I knew there was virtue in being a good guy, and I played that role for many years."

"Can you tell me about your wife and daughter?" I ask, choosing that moment to shift the conversation to something a little more uncomfortable for him.

He looks away, his jaw tightening. He suddenly appears on the verge of choking up.

"We were having a lot of problems," he manages while holding back his tears. "My daughter was seven at that point. We'd been fighting for a while about money, disagreements, how to parent her. We were very different people who never should have had a child together, and then we each started taking out our frustration on each other. I yelled, she screamed all the worst things you can imagine."

"Did you ever hit her?"

"We had one big fight. She threw plates at me. I threw plates at her. One hit her head. She refused to go to the hospital because she didn't want to press charges. We were oil and vinegar. I was the worst version of myself with her, and I believe she was the worst version of herself with me."

Now he starts to twiddle his thumbs, one over the other. His cuticles are pushed back, neat, just like everything else about him.

"But you're not here to talk about what happened with them, are you?"

"Not exactly, but we're just getting to know each other, right?"

"I'd prefer to not, I'm sure that Donald filled you in on how I ended up here. My own mistakes that came out after what my wife did, but if you want me to talk about my uncle, getting me to open up about my wife is not the way to go. It's raising my blood pressure already and I'm just warning you it's not going to lead anywhere good."

He remains calm as he says this, detached somehow. With anyone else, I would've figured that they were full of crap and lies, but with him, it was different. Instinctively I knew what he was doing, compartmentalizing, putting his feelings in separate little boxes to not feel them so strongly. That's why detectives sometimes make jokes at the most gruesome crime scenes. It's not that they don't care, they do, it's that laughter and detachment is really the only way to deal with all the darkness.

"Ok, tell me about your uncle," I say.

"He was just someone that I saw quite a lot when I was growing up and we stayed in touch as adults. We're very close in age and we're more like brothers than anything else. We would go out to get drinks together. We had the same similar sense of humor. He complained about his job a lot, but he did nothing to change it."

"Where did he work?" I ask.

"The same place he worked all of his life, the Boyden paper company out in north Portland. He did sales for them, went to conventions, trade shows, different businesses, spent a lot of time on the road, traveled maybe two weeks out of the month. It made relationships difficult."

"Does he have a family?"

“No. He was married for a little while and then they got divorced. He's not the nicest guy to be around when he drinks, and he's been drinking a lot more. All throughout the years as I went through my various changes in jobs and entrepreneurial ventures, I kept asking him why he kept working at the same place, and he said job security. He said that it's the only thing that makes any sense to him to do. I don't even think he had a resume and I don't know if he ever knew how to write a cover letter. That was so different from me because I had about ten different careers. Started out working retail, bartended, worked as a life-guard at a community pool, groundskeeper at a country club then got into real estate and financial services, which eventually got me in trouble, but first made me a whole lot of money.

"I tried to give him some advice. Every time I changed jobs, David called me a flake. He said no one will want to hire me again, but the thing is that in today's economy, fluidity of labor, the ability to move and go to better positions and better jobs is really the only leverage you have to make money. If somebody pays you a couple of bucks over minimum wage here, you apply some-where else and lie and say they pay you five bucks instead. Then the new offer comes in for six or seven dollars above minimum wage. Then you work there a year, maybe a year and a half. You do the same thing. I switched fields, which perhaps isn't advisable. But without doing so, I would've never found out about making loans. Loan processing, and the lucrative business that it afforded me, even before I started embezzling money which, I agree, was a terrible mistake."

The nonchalance with which he speaks is disarming. Most people would be embarrassed, lost, denying their culpability. It's almost like he's above embarrassment. He's admitting his fault. He's doing his time. I know that when he gets out, he's going to follow his own advice to a T. Hopefully minus the embezzlement.

"I don't want to blame my wife entirely because I had plenty of toys. My garage was full of them but despite how much money I made, we couldn't live within our means. Initially, we lived on barely anything. Then we got addicted to buying things, vacations, houses, cars. It was nice to have a few new things. Despite what people say about loving material goods, you can actually do that.

"It wasn't just the buying that made my heart skip. It was driving my Porsche Cayenne around town. It was seeing my wife in her Mercedes. It was taking those vacations to Italy. Flying first class, staying in five-star hotels, we had made it. The luxury items are better. Better made, better cared for. I didn't always know that as a poor kid growing up.

"David, on the other hand, made fun of me a lot. When I ended up in this place, he really laid into me telling me *'didn't I know that you can't buy happiness by buying expensive things.'* All that usual crap. He lived very conservatively within his means. His means weren't much. He said he didn't want anything, but I could tell that he did. He just couldn't imagine seeing himself owning something like that.

He had a lot of hang-ups about money. He didn't believe he deserved it. It's a common problem, actually. It's one of the reasons why people overspend and try to go back to zero when they win the lottery or anything like that. In my case, I overspent because I just got greedy. Simple as that."

"What are you going to do after you get out of here?" I asked.

"There're some limitations about the financial instruments that I can sell and participate in during my probation. I'm going to look into it and figure out what I can and can't do. Working is the only thing I really know. That's why I've been working so hard inside. Working out, following a schedule, and a routine. Without it, you're just lost. The depression gets the worst of you. I'm going to figure out what my limitations are legally and then reinvent myself again. What else is there to do? I did my time. I'm not going to be embarrassed by this the rest of my life. I made mistakes, but so what? Right? I don't have to pay for them forever, unlike my wife."

Then suddenly a wave of emotion overwhelms him, and he breaks down. His shoulders moving up and down as he cries. I put my arm slightly around his left one and pat him on the back, trying to calm him down but he continues to sob. The kids around us look at him as if he has lost his mind. The little boy asks why he's crying.

"He's just very sad," I say. "Something very bad happened to him."

"Something very bad happened to my daddy too," the little boy says, his eyes glistening in the light. "But it's okay. He'll be home soon and then he's going to play with me again."

"That's good." I give him and his father and mother a knowing nod.

Up until Victor mentioned his family he'd been a practical man who had his head screwed on straight as they like to say. If someone in his position were to ask me for advice as to what to do after incarceration, that's exactly what I would say.

"Just move on with your life. You paid for your misdeed. There's no need for dwelling on the past. Get a job. Do something self-actualizing. If it's making money, do that. If it's volunteering, do that."

Victor gasps for breath and takes a few deep inhalations before wiping the last of the tears away.

"I'm sorry. It came over me."

"No need to apologize," I say.

"The thing is that I never expected her to do that." He shakes his head. "I've never even heard of a so-called family annihilator who was a woman like that, who would take it out on her own daughter to get back at me. I mean, a mother just killing a daughter, yes, but she loved her so much. She killed her to get back at me the way that all those other famous cases like Chris Watts, who killed his two daughters and his wife in Colorado.

“My wife wasn't having an affair, she wasn't going to start a new life somewhere else. She just killed our daughter and herself to cause me pain. She was going through a lot of depression and had mentioned suicide a number of times, but I never took it seriously because when we had those fights, it just was total chaos. Never once did I think that she would do what she did and then she did. It changed everything."

"I'm so sorry," I say reaching over and giving his hand a squeeze.

He swallows hard and I see the way his Adam's apple moves up and down, pushing away the pain.

“Things sometimes happen in life, and you can blame yourself, but you can also try to move on. It's probably some terrible advice that I offer but it's the only thing that I can think of at this moment."

"You're not here to talk about her though, right? You want to know about David."

I gave him a nod.

"What do you want to know?"

Chapter 25

There was so much that I wanted to know about David Trincia and yet, I had no idea where to start. Was he willing to tell me everything, every last detail, or were there some things that he was going to hold back because he was, after all, family, and probably the only family he had left?

"Why did you decide to come forward?" I ask. Focusing not so much on Victor's uncle, but his own motivations, whatever they may be.

"I trusted Donald, despite the fact that he was instrumental in putting me away. We developed a friendship. He came to see me a little bit because I don't know, I guess we were probably more alike than he would ever want to admit. I decided to tell him. I hadn't investigated any of it myself, not really, not until after Donald took an interest. David and I were drinking a lot that night when he told me about the deaths, the murders."

Victor corrects himself. He's looking straight at me now, face completely relaxed, no tension in his jaw or neck muscles. His expression reminds me of the way that a man would talk to a good friend of his, not putting on airs, not trying to be boastful or impress me with anything. Just telling me what it is that he had heard.

"David had never mentioned anything like that to me before and that was the only time that he did. We would go on these binges together. We wouldn't see each other for one or two months and when we'd reconnect, we'd go to a bar, then another, and another, and just get really wasted, all night long. At one point, he came back home with me to my house. He was visiting the area for work. He started walking around the place talking about how ridiculous it was, how big and fancy, and how there were people starving in the world and that I didn't deserve any of it.

"He was really angry that night. I tried to calm him down, but I was pretty drunk myself. At some point, he just started talking. He said that his life should have been like mine, that he should have had this big house, and the pretty wife, and the nice kid, but his kids were grown now and they were ungrateful. They took everything for granted. They didn't realize how much he had sacrificed. Frankly, I remember thinking that I didn't think he'd sacrificed that much. He worked the same job his whole life."

"He never put himself outside his comfort zone."

"Yes, he didn't really-- That was his choice, right?"

Victor takes pauses for a moment, inhales deeply, and exhales, his nostrils flaring.

"I need a break," he says. "Can you buy me a Coke?"

I get up and put a few coins in the vending machine. $2 for a can of Coke. Inflation seemed to have hit the vending machine soda industry hard. I smile to myself. I'm pretty certain that since he had told me this much, he'd tell me more. What I'm not certain about is whether I can believe any of it.

The can of soda makes a loud clinking sound when it falls to the bottom of the machine. I hand it to Victor, who takes extra care in releasing the gas to make sure that it doesn't explode all over the place.

"You want any sweets or chips?" I ask.

He shakes his head, "No. Sticking to a strict diet here, I'm almost close to my goal weight."

"What about the Coke?" I ask punching E9, as my mouth starts to salivate for the sour onion chips that I'm about to taste.

"I can't give up all my vices in here. I don't know if you know it but having this conversation with you is really raising my blood pressure. It's not exactly something I enjoy talking about, even though Donald seems to think it's the only thing that I need to discuss. Here we are, I'm appeasing some of my anxiety with a little bit of Coke. Is that so bad?"

"No, not at all," I give him a smile. I pop a chip into my mouth--and chew with my lips closed, waiting for him to speak first. Instead, he just plays with the tab of the Coke can, pressing it down and back up again nervously.

"What did he tell you that night?" I asked.

"Told me too much stuff I never wanted to hear, stuff I could never forget."

"Like what?" I ask after a long pause again.

He was going on and on about how I had too much stuff that I didn't need and he didn't have any. He said he'd missed out on life. Like I said, he was traveling again for work and that always brought him down. We drank a little too much and he started walking back and forth, ranting and raving in my living room. I kept telling him to be quiet because my kid was asleep upstairs, but he wouldn't shut up until he sat down on the recliner and just buried his head in his hands.

"He started to sob, and he told me that he had a demon inside of him who made him do bad things. I thought he had lost his mind. I had no idea what he was talking about, but he just kept going on and on about it. How he didn't mean to do it, but the demon made him do it. He was afraid and he never knew when this demon was going to strike and make him do bad things."

He takes a sip of the Coke and then looks straight up at me.

"That's when he told me."

"Told you what?" I asked.

"That's when he told me about killing those three people, one of them being a kid."

I stare at him waiting for him to say more, but he seems to need a moment to think about everything. He just looks lost. I know the broad details of what he told Donald, the basics of what he was going to say, the names, how the story was revealed, but hearing it for the first time and seeing its effect on Victor himself, even all of this time, is difficult for me to take it all in stride. Now, suddenly, I understand why Donald was so adamant that this guy was telling the truth. There's nothing people pleasing about him, especially when it comes to this story. In fact, he seems to want to move away, as far away from it as possible.

He doesn't want anyone to know, and he doesn't want to keep retelling the story to strangers because this is his close friend and relative after all. "What did he tell you exactly about the people that he killed and how did he say it?

"He told me the locations of three bodies. He just kept saying the demon made him do it. I remember, even though I was in a drunken stupor, I had enough sense to pull out a piece of paper when he wasn't looking and write it down. I almost got caught but I managed to hide in the bathroom."

"Why did you do that?" I ask.

"I had to, I wanted to make sure that he wasn't making this up."

"Was he?"

"I figured if I knew these locations which he had told me and I looked them up and there were no bodies found there, then there you go. He's one of those crazies who confesses to crimes that he didn't commit."

"Is that what happened?"

"No, the next morning, nursing a very bad hangover, I made myself some eggs and the blackest coffee possible. I typed the scribbles into Google, the cross streets that he had mentioned, the towns."

"And?"

"And those are the exact spots where the bodies were found," Victor breaks down. "There was a little boy who was in preschool, Langley Daniels, a teenage runaway, Bree Xander, and a

25-year-old grad student, Frida Wolf. Their names and bodies were identified, but no one knew who did it."

"Is there any possibility that he was aware of these cases, and the fact that they were still unsolved, and decided to confess to them?"

"Perhaps. I thought about that," Victor says hanging his head.

"The thing is that I kept waiting for him to bring it up again, but the only thing he ever asked me was later the next afternoon, he asked if he had said anything crazy the night before. I said, 'No,' and he didn't elaborate. He often bluffs about stuff when he is drunk, and I guess that's what he figured had happened. He didn't realize that he'd told me anything."

I lean over away from the table, pressing my fingers against the Formica top.

"How come you never told anyone about this, before Donald?" I ask. " I mean you had plenty of time and opportunity. You could have just gone to the police station. Isn't it a little bit convenient that the cases were Donald's."

Without missing a beat, he says, "I didn't even want to tell him."

That takes me by surprise.

"What are you talking about?" I ask.

"I wasn't going to tell anyone. I mean the murders were unsolved, but the victims were identified, and the families at least knew where they were and what had happened to them. David and I are still close. For a long time I thought that it was just something that he had imagined or maybe just said because he was bored and wanted to make himself more important. He was the one who did better at school. He was the one who was a straight shooter. Never had a DUI, never stole money from anyone, but he didn't have a nice house or any of that stuff and I knew it was bothering him."

"Maybe he just admitted something to me that he shouldn't have. Maybe I had imagined the whole thing. I knew I needed to stop drinking at that point. I didn't want to think about it. I didn't want to go tell the police. I didn't want to be involved with it at all."

"What made you change your mind?"

"Being in here, sober. Just living my life on the edge. Donald was the only one who came to see me. I mean David did, a few times, but once it was inconvenient, he didn't bother anymore."

"Are you sure you're not just mad at him?" I ask. "Mad that he isn't stopping by anymore?"

"No, absolutely not," he says.

"Donald and I started talking. I asked him about the cases that he had. He started mentioning that there were a number of unsolved ones that were bothering him. Suddenly, I saw another glimpse into who and what he is, and I realized that it's not just the family and the victim who are affected. It's everyone involved who ends up with no answers to all these questions. I thought about it for some time. He hadn't mentioned any of his cases to me in great detail. Then I just decided to go for it and tell him what I knew even if I didn't know much."

"What happened?" I ask.

"They ended up being his cases. I was as shocked as anyone. It was ridiculous almost. I wasn't sure what to do with any of that information. I just told him what I knew. That's it."

One of the guards steps closer to the table to say that visiting hours are over. If it weren't for that, I feel like I've just gotten started talking about this, but Victor seems relieved, unwilling perhaps to say more or to delve further into any of this.

"Thank you for your time," I say, as Victor gets up to leave.

"Thanks for coming. Not exactly the most pleasant of visits, but it is what it is."

He doesn't offer me additional help. He doesn't invite me to come by again, though I'm not sure that he would reject the visit entirely. Talking to him in person, he definitely seemed credible, but at the same time, I wonder if this has anything to do with wishful thinking. For instance, did he speak to Donald and want to help him so much and so desperately that he decided to throw him a few breadcrumbs?

I don't want to go so far as to say that he had looked up Donald's cases and told him that David had confessed to those murders because that would be too easy to prove.

What would be the reason for him to frame his uncle and good friend? But if I assume that he's telling the truth about David's drunken night and the admissions that he'd made while he was on the bender then I have to believe that the locations of the bodies are also correct and were also something that he had admitted to.

What does that mean then? That's something that I have no way to figure out. I get back to the car no more certain about the truth than when I had arrived. I know that Donald is going to look at me with his eyes full of hope expecting me to solve all his problems and before I see him I have to make up my mind.

What do I believe exactly? For one, I believe that Victor is mostly truthful. I don't think he would be framing his uncle, especially with three murders for no reason whatsoever but to please a retired FBI agent.

If I believe that he's truthfully recounting what he heard. But I still have to figure out whether David had confessed to what he had actually done or whether he's one of those people who confesses to murders that he had nothing to do with for a little bit of attention.

The likelihood of the second is waning, of course, because the truth is that he only said it once and he didn't come forward to the police. It's also unclear whether he even knew that he had told Victor in the first place. It gives us a little bit of an edge, not much though, and there are still so many other things to figure out.

Chapter 26

Anthony came home with a heavy head. Even calling his father's house *his home* made him sick to his stomach, and now he had to live there all the time. He was angry, pissed off, hateful of the world and everything that had happened. His mother was gone, and his father was acting like it was no big deal. His stepmother, once an ally, had completely checked out and refused to talk about his mother in any capacity whatsoever.

Instead of talking about any of this in normal tones, everybody walked around on tiptoes. On this particular Friday afternoon, Anthony had decided to invite his girlfriend, Evelyn Ware, over to his new house. He knew he was supposed to ask first. She begged him to because his father was not a fan of guests, but he knew what the answer would be if he had asked. Instead, he lied to

Evelyn and when she'd showed up with him on the bus, she knew immediately that she was not wanted.

His father's eyes narrowed, and he pulled his son aside,

"You're going to have to ask her to leave because you never asked my permission to invite her."

"She's here already," Anthony said.

"Yes, that's not my problem."

"Can't she just stay for an hour or two before dinner? What would be the problem?"

"The problem is that you don't like to follow rules and I can't have that. You have to know your place in this house. Otherwise, you won't have one."

It wasn't uncommon for his father to speak to him this way. Theodor Rydell thought that he was being stern in trying to teach his son how to be an adult, but in reality, Anthony was a kid who had just lost his mother and had never done anything to rebel in any way whatsoever. He just wanted to relive a little bit of the past that he'd had in his old home. As was to be expected, an argument ensued, only it wasn't Anthony who got mad.

It was his father who yelled at him, told him what an ungrateful kid he was and that his mother had spoiled him rotten and now he had to pay for the consequences of all of that. Evelyn had wisely called her mother and got picked up after less than half an hour of being in that house.

"I love you, but I can't stay," she said, giving him a kiss on the cheek. "If you're ever allowed out, come visit me, or we'll just see each other at school."

As he watched her walk away, he realized that he was losing more and more of his life for no reason. With his mother's disappearance and then murder, he had lost the most important thing in his life.

Now his father was taking all the other things he cared about. What were his options exactly? He couldn't move out and the cops had no clues about who had this.

Anthony thought he did, though. He'd been doing some of his own investigation reaching out to Detective Kaitlyn Carr, who seemed to be interested in helping him and looking through his dad's emails and text messages when he wasn't looking.

This is how he would get his revenge. He would find out the truth about where his dad was that night and uncover it all.

"When are you going to wash that purple gunk out of your hair?" Theodor asked when they sat down for dinner. "The answer better be tonight. I don't want to see it anymore. Boys aren't supposed to have purple hair."

"Technically, no one is supposed to have purple hair."

Anthony started to say but Melinda, his stepmother, shook her head slightly and looked at him with a great deal of sympathy. The older he got, the more Anthony had realized why his mother and his father never stayed together and the more thankful he was that his mother was strong enough to walk away.

His stepmother wasn't and here she was trapped in the house with a man who would yell at her, call her names, and occasionally hit her, to make a point. Still she stayed, supposedly for the children, but her life became smaller and smaller. Only a few years ago, she had a job and volunteered at the kid's school and had friends, but now she wasn't even allowed to do that.

"Your mother's going to be cremated and we'll get her ashes next week," Theodor said taking a big bite of his brisket. "Think about if you want to have any service for her, but you'll have to organize it."

“Cremated?" Anthony bit his lower lip.

He had watched enough crime shows to know that very little evidence survives with cremation inside a 4,000-degree oven when a human body is turned into ash and fragments of bones. If he had wanted to find out what really happened to his mom, he would have to stop this from happening.

"But mom did not want to be cremated."

"It's a lot more expensive to have a real burial. The funeral home and all that stuff. I don't have the money for that. If you do, you're more than welcome to do it, but it's thousands of dollars."

"What about her body and the DNA? Maybe they'll find out something."

"They took all the samples they wanted. They're releasing the body to the family," Theodor said.

"Maybe in the future, they'll invent something that will allow them to find out something else. They didn't have the DNA until the early 90s. If this case goes cold--"

"Look, that's not my problem, Anthony. It's very sad what happened to your mom but to be honest with you, she probably brought this on herself. She lived a bit of a reckless life."

"No, she didn't. She didn't see any men. She was a hairdresser and that's it. I don't know what you're talking about."

"There are rumors, Anthony. Rumors I try to keep from you but clearly, you now need to know. All the money that your mom made was not entirely from her salon. There was another kind of business that she was involved with."

"Even if that's true, and I'm not saying it is, she's still my mom and I deserve to know what happened, we all deserve to know what had happened. The guy who did this deserves to be in prison for the rest of his life if not the electric chair. Right?"

Theodor hesitated for a moment, taking a bite and chewing slowly.

"Things happen between adults Anthony. You don't fully understand the details."

Was this a hint of some kind? Anthony wondered.

Was his father trying to tell him that despite having an alibi he knew what had happened to his mother? Maybe was part of it?

"We can't have her cremated," Anthony said. "They don't know who did this and they may find evidence on her body later."

"How is that my problem? We have to do something with her now and I can't afford a burial. We have a trip to Disney World that I'm still going to be paying off for a while."

This was a trip that Anthony was not going on. It was reserved entirely for the primary family, and Anthony was staying home with the pets, which was all perfectly fine with him, anyway. His thoughts raced as he tried to figure out a way to get his father to change his mind.

"What if you put it on the credit card and I get a job and I pay it off? Maybe one of those 0% promotional rate cards?"

"That's going to eat into our credit."

"Dad, please. This is very important. We'll get the cheapest coffin they have but we can't have her cremated. That will destroy whatever evidence is on her body. If they hadn't found it yet, maybe they'll have something that they'll need to confirm in the future. I've watched a lot of these shows and that's how it happens. But there may still be some sort of evidence and we can't destroy it."

"You watch too much television, Anthony. We're going to have to work on that," Theodor said with a huff.

He got up to get another beer from the fridge, but Anthony secretly started smiling to himself.

At least he didn't say no. At least there was still a chance.

Chapter 27

Anthony had gotten into the habit of tracking me down or running into me when I least expected it. On this occasion, he must have followed me from my hotel to the coffee shop across the street. Perhaps he even waited out in the parking lot until I came out in the morning.

"You really can't do this," I say to him, standing in line to get two coffees to go.

"I need to talk to you about my case."

"You can call me, you can text me. You can't just show up anytime you want."

"But you don't understand," he says, looking flustered, his eyes bewildered. "My dad, he wants to have Mom cremated and that's going to destroy everything."

I stare at him, pausing slightly. When the barista asks me for my order, I can't remember.

"I'd like a Grande latte with oat milk and a tall cappuccino," I mumble.

While we wait, I ask him if he wants anything. He mutters no and waits with me at the counter with the rest of the patrons.

"Ok, tell me what's going on," I say, realizing that I'm not very good at setting and keeping boundaries. This isn't my case, but I feel responsible for it anyway, especially to him, especially given that I was the one who found her.

"My dad told me yesterday that he's going to have her cremated, but I know she wouldn't want that. I mean, she would have if she had died under natural causes, but she wouldn't have wanted that in this situation, with everything so unsolved."

"What are you trying to tell me?" I whisper. A couple of the people look back at us and I pull him closer to the window.

"I don't know what to say," he mumbles.

"Do you think that your father is involved?"

"I didn't really before, but he just seems so unreasonable. It's like he doesn't want anyone to find out."

"Did he explain his reasons in any way?"

"Yes, he said it would cost a lot of money that he doesn't want to spend. He's going to Disney World and it's going to cost a lot as well. This is just an unexpected expense and cremation is a lot cheaper. The thing is that it's like he doesn't even care that no one knows what had happened. He blames her. He thinks she's the problem. He said something about her being an escort, but there was no evidence of it. No other cell phone, no one contacting her. No emails, no other accounts. I really looked, I'm not trying to cover her tracks. I want to find out the truth."

"I can see that, Anthony. I'm really sorry." When our drinks come up, I ask him if he wants to sit down and talk, but he says no.

"Somewhere private."

"How about my car?"

He nods. When we get inside, he tenses up. He doesn't say a word, just stares into the distance, saying nothing.

"I don't know if my father had anything to do with this. I know that he doesn't care. I want to believe that that's why he wants to get her cremated. Just the cheapest way to dispose of her as possible. But he doesn't understand how important the body is for evidence. I mean, who knows what other things they're going to find out in the future? DNA didn't exist until what, forty years ago? Now they need less and less evidence to even find it. For the longest time it was just handprints, footprints. Body fluids. That was it."

"Yes, you're right," I say. "I guess I could talk to him, but I'm not sure it's going to do you any good. How about this? I'll talk to the detectives to the people and the investigators in charge. I'll tell them your concerns. Maybe they can put a lien on the body and postpone the cremation if they think they might collect evidence in the future."

"You can do that?"

"I can try. You know that I'm not officially on this case. It's just a courtesy that they're even talking to me at all or sharing any details. But so far, they don't have much. I can ask if they've done any further research into her possibly being an escort, but it seems like you're pretty certain that she had nothing to do with that. Is that correct?"

"I really looked everywhere. I found a few of her old email accounts, like her maiden name ones that she hasn't used in a while. There was nothing there either. They're all dormant."

"That's good to know," I say. "No evidence is sometimes evidence as well, but like with everything else, I can't make any promises. You know that, right? Cases like this are notoriously difficult to solve."

"There's something else. She had this bag with her," he says. "I've been looking for it everywhere, but I can't find it. It was a small bright red cross body with leather and chain straps. She often had an over the shoulder bag that she put it into, but she always had it like a wallet. She had pictures of me in there from when I was a baby and other things."

"Like what?" I asked.

"Credit cards, a locket."

"What kind of locket?"

"She used to wear it around her neck, but the chain broke. It was a little gold locket, heart shaped. I gave it to her when I was six years old for Mother's Day. My grandma helped me pick it out. The chain broke half a year ago or so and she kept meaning to get it repaired, but I guess she never did, but she was always carrying it around with her. I know because once, when I was looking for a credit card to pay for something online, there it was. She told me that she wanted to keep it close."

"This red purse, she always had it with her?"

"Yes. Always. I thought for sure it would be with her body, but they never returned it to us. They never processed it. I don't know if it's still kept as evidence, but can you ask the detectives about it? I would really like to have it back. Especially if they have collected whatever they need from it. It's really special because my mom loved it."

"Yes, I understand. Okay, I'll ask."

"Thank you so much for helping with all of this. The few times I went over there, they just shut down and wouldn't answer any questions.

Said everything was private, but it's hard to know if they're even working on anything at all."

"I know. The thing is that you have to check up on cases but sometimes, in some situations, detectives have more information that they just don't want to reveal to you."

"Why?"

"Because it would compromise it, because you might let it slip to someone or it might get out, and the best tool they have for finding out the truth is to keep a big portion of the case secret until the bad guy is put on trial, when it's all revealed. Up until that point they don't want anything public. That's why they seem like they're shut down, but at the same time, it's important to keep in touch. Calling, checking up, reminding them that somebody cares, and someone should be looking into any possible leads."

"Okay. That makes me feel better."

"I'll ask about the purse. I'll talk about your dad's cremation request, but I have to let you know if they don't have a good reason to hold the body, if they feel like they've collected all evidence, then you and your father would be next of kin since you're underage. So, it might be good for you to try to talk him out of it."

"Okay, I'll try, but he's one stubborn SOB."

"Yes, I'm kind of getting that sense."

Chapter 28

I returned to our room and handed Luke his lukewarm coffee with an apology. He shrugged and smiled, put in the microwave to heat up, grumbling a little bit at how things in the microwave don't taste as good. I filled him in about what happened with Anthony, and we talked a little bit about my interview with Victor yesterday. The whole process took almost the whole day, and our vacation is quickly coming to a close with very little rest or relaxation, and the cases that are unsolved seem even more impossible and unlikely to be closed anytime soon.

"What do you think about getting married next summer?" he asks.

We have danced around the topic of getting engaged, but I'm not one for an official proposal and neither is he.

"I do want to marry you. You know that, right?" He's lying on his back, his head propped up by his arm, leaning on the headboard. The hotel is nothing fancy, but it does have a little patio with tall pine trees outside, they give it a bucolic feel.

"I was going to take you to some romantic place and ask you if you want to make it official, but we were never really anywhere like that this whole time, so I figured now is as good a time as any."

I hesitate, shifting my weight from one side of the chair to another.

"You want to marry me, right?"

"I do," I say. "Though, I wouldn't mind an actual proposal."

"I'd have to be able to see you at least once in a while in order to make that happen."

"Yeah, I get it," I laugh.

"Next time we're on the beach or back in Kansas?" he asks. "On the farm."

"I don't know. Beach sounds nice."

"Of course, we can always do a honeymoon."

"Now you're talking," he smiles.

"Well, in any case, my family will fly anywhere to see you, so it's no problem really. They're not exactly convinced that we'll get married, but we'll show them." I smile at him and then climb on top of him and give him a big kiss on the lips.

"I'll marry you anytime, anywhere, but I'm not one for big celebrations."

"No, just going to be our family. Nothing major," I hesitate.

"You're thinking about your sister, right?"

"Yeah, and mom," I admit. "She's still not exactly okay after everything that she has gone through. I mean, we're so happy to have her back in whatever form, but she's different now. That light in her eyes, it's a little bit gone."

He grabs my hand, intertwines his fingers with mine. He's been there through it all, searching for her back in my hometown of Big Bear Lake and looking for answers in all the wrong places.

"Despite what had happened to her and how much she was hurt by the man who took her, she's one of the lucky ones. She's back at home."

"How are things between her and your mom?"

"I haven't talked to either one of them that much. I called Violet and she never answered the phone. Mom has filled me in about it on a few occasions. She said she's very helpful at home, doesn't go out, is happy to go to school virtually this year and just stay away from everyone. She's become kind of a shut-in."

"That's good, right? I mean."

"Well, my mom is happy," I say sitting down on the edge of the bed. "But the thing is, Violet is not a shut-in. Violet is the one who wanted to go to private school and live with me in LA. She's independent, outgoing. She wanted to study art. She signed up to be that apprentice. She signed up to learn how to make tattoos. She's somebody who lives life on the edge. Before this happened, she would have never entertained the idea of virtual school or staying home with mom in our old house on the lake for so long, but it's like she's completely changed."

"She's afraid, Kaitlyn. She's afraid of what happened to her. She's trying to keep away from everyone and everything."

"I know, and maybe it's a coping mechanism that will work for the time being but what about when it stops working? I just don't want her to stay that way. You know, at some point, you're afraid to go outside and it feels good but, eventually, just becomes this, the world becomes this scary place where you just try to escape, and you stay home all the time because you start to fear your own shadow."

"Are you speaking from experience?" Luke asks.

I give him a slight nod.

"I was much older than Violet was and nothing that terrible had happened to me, but I lost my father, whether it was suicide or murder or whatever; he was gone, and I was there and I saw his body and all that blood all over the walls. I just became a recluse after that. I went through the motions, went to school but never talked to anyone, never really bothered making friends, just detached from life. It's like, I didn't think I deserved to have a good time. Then, when I started working for the LAPD, I didn't have time to do anything else. It was just work and home and that's it. The only thing I ever wanted was to get a pet, and I wasn't sure that I'd be home to take care of it, so that never happened. Violet associates me with what happened to her because I was the one that rescued her and I know that she doesn't mean to push me away, but that's exactly what she's doing. I know that I need to go see her. I can't just call. I can't just text. I need to spend some real time with her, but this vacation is taking all of my days off and, frankly, it hasn't been much of a vacation, and I'm sorry about that."

"Look, I know that you're leaving this place with more questions than you got answers to, but the reason you came, the reason that he wrote that in his letter, it's still there."

"What do you mean?" I ask.

"You came to find out what happened to your father, right?"

I give him a slight nod.

"Donald told you?"

We haven't talked about it much. I don't know what to say.

"Do you believe that he was telling you the truth?"

"Yes."

"And the video?"

My mind flashes to the image of two guys talking in a messy hotel room. One of them is Max Powell. He's telling the other guy with a receding hairline to kill my father and make it look like suicide. He threatens the other guy, Deacon Omni, and says that he better kill my father or he will kill his whole family.

"I don't think Donald would make that up. He was working for the FBI then and Max was a higher up in the cartel. This piece of evidence just came up when they were recording things for the case against him, but I still don't know where Max Powell or Deacon Omni went. I mean, the cartel could have killed him. He's gone. How would I ever find him?"

"You know his name. You know what he looks like. You know the associations."

"The cartel could have killed him, or maybe he just took the money and disappeared himself."

"Yes, those are all possibilities. But what if I helped you find out the truth? I mean, I'm still a special agent for the FBI. I have some time and resources. I'm not going to work there for long, Kaitlyn. If you need my help, you have to let me know."

Luke and I have not talked about the situation with my father much. I've gone through the details, but I wondered if he had done some research.

"Have you looked them up? Did you find anything?"

“I did a little bit of digging. I found a few pictures, some reports that he was under investigation, but I'm going to have to talk to the people working on those cases to get any more details. It's not all in files online, as you know.”

I nod.

"And I don't want to just bring up your father for no reason. All I'm saying is that this trip wasn't a total waste. We came here because Donald needed help. You helped him and he told you about your father and what happened."

"What might have happened," I correct him. "You really think it's suicide after all this time?"

"Or was it a forced suicide? Was someone pointing a gun at his head and threatening you and your mom and your little sister who were about to come home?"

I burst into tears. Big sobs and thick droplets run down my cheeks. I hadn't cried like this in a really long time, especially for my father, who had become just an asterisk in my story. Someone I had loved and had a complicated relationship with, and who committed suicide because of his various entanglements in drug deals.

"What about our vacation?" I ask through the tears. I laugh, and he laughs too. A little comic relief goes a long way.

"Well, since I'm marrying you, and not anyone else, I guess it's to be expected. Here I am enjoying a trip to the Pacific Northwest and set up hiking and taking pictures in front of waterfalls and green pine trees. We're neck-deep in dead bodies and unsolved murders."

Luke's right. I did come here for one thing, the promise of finding out what had happened to my father. I guess in that regard, I did.

"I don't know what to do about my sister, though," I say, "or all these unsolved murders. How do I help Anthony?"

"Go talk to Captain Carville. Fill him in on what you heard. I don't know. Maybe they have more of a clue. Maybe it was her ex-husband or boyfriend. Maybe it's not as complicated as it seems."

"Yes, maybe." I nod.

"What about Victor?"

"That's up to you. Trust your gut. Any ideas on how you feel about what he said to you?"

"I don't know," I say. "I hate to say, but I feel like he's telling the truth. This is his closest family member and friend. He seems to really not want to believe that he did the things that he said he did. As far as Victor is concerned, I believe that he's telling the truth."

"I think you just go and talk to Donald. Tell him your thoughts. Go from there. We have to get back tomorrow. You have work and everything else. There's nothing else that you can really do here."

"It just feels like I'm leaving everything so up in the air. No answers for all of these questions."

"We can come back. You can come back. We can go from there."

Chapter 29

My thoughts are as quick as molasses when I get into the car. My intention is to drive to the station and talk to Captain Carville and the other detectives in charge of the case. Everything they tell me, if they tell me anything, would be entirely at their own discretion and completely unnecessary. I'm an outsider with no real connection to the case except for being the person who found the body. I've given them multiple statements, but my involvement with Anthony might set them off and get them to clam up.

I have yet to talk to Donald about my meeting with Victor. He's itching to hear my thoughts and has left me numerous messages. Before I talk to him, however, I really want to make up my own mind, pay attention to my gut, my instincts about whether or not Victor is telling the truth. I don't want to fall into the trap or will myself into believing something that I really don't just because it would make Donald's day and he'd finally have someone at his side.

The rain fell heavier today, as if it were being poured out of buckets instead of the steady misting it had been doing for the majority of my trip. It seemed to not end, no matter how far I drove or how long I waited for it to stop. I had looked up a few hikes and wanted to take one last one before I went back down to Southern California. The places around here are astoundingly beautiful, and so different from what I'm used to seeing. I haven't seen nearly as much of the natural world as I wanted. The rains, and my lack of adequate clothing have really gotten in the way. I have an umbrella, of course, but it was like God was playing a joke on me, tossing it all around with the wind and having it turned inside out just on my way to the parking lot.

It was barely nine in the morning, but it could have been twilight and although I had the heat blasting in the car, it wasn't doing much against the dampness of my wet jacket. Everybody around here seemed to wear waterproof REI hiking gear, just walking around, and I knew I needed to get myself one as well, but my flight back was tomorrow. There was no real point since it hardly ever rains in LA, so I would just have to suffer through being a little wet today hoping that I didn't get sick in the process. I took the long way to the station, looping around multiple streets, even though the GPS kept redirecting me the right way to go. I just didn't quite want to get to the station so quickly and needed time to figure out what to say.

As I waited for the red light to change, my thoughts returned to Big Bear and my sister Violet, and my mom who I haven't talked to nearly as much as I should have; we've always had a complicated relationship. She was difficult to get along with and kept too much to herself. She thought I was a bad influence on Violet; and now that Violet is back, she is back to protecting her too much from me. I don't have proof of any of this, it's just a feeling. And it isn't like I have tried that hard to reach out either. I had certain answers about what happened to our father, answers that I knew my mom would probably reject since she was adamant about it being suicide, answers that were probably too difficult for Violet to process in her fragile state. After having survived a kidnapping and sexual assault, the depths and the details of which I still did not know, she didn't need to have this old wound torn open again.

I hope my mom encouraged her to go to

therapy and to talk to someone, a professional, about what had happened, but I don't even know if that much had happened. Ever since I found her in the desert at that psycho's house, I have pulled back from my own family, as much as they have kept away from me. It is almost as if it is too hard to see them, to talk to them because they reminded me so much of everything that we have experienced. Instead of pulling together, sticking by one another, I went on this trip with Luke, got busy with work and cases, all in an effort to compartmentalize the pain that I have felt over the mistakes that I had made in investigating her case, in finding who killed her friend, and everything else that had happened.

Luke is right about one thing; I do have to decide how far I want to pursue finding out the truth about my father. Do I find Max Powell? Do I just let it go?

We haven't talked about it much, but Luke has made it perfectly clear that he has no plans of staying in the FBI for the rest of his working life. I admire his ability to just announce that and stick to it; it's not easy. He seems to know that investigating crimes and working the hours that he works is not sustainable for him. It doesn't make him happy. He has done enough and now, before burning out, before succumbing to a life of drinking and numbing yourself to try to escape it all, he can just admit that it's too much and he'd rather have a good family and be there for his kids, the kids that he supposes we will have together.

I want that with him or the idea of it, I've never really considered having children with anyone before. I can't even imagine me as a mom, participating in the parent-teacher association, hanging out with other moms.

What would that even be like? What would we have in common? But I do want to be with him, and I feel like he tames my worst vices. He makes me feel good about myself and he makes me want to be a better person. I don't feel anxious around him. In fact, it's the complete opposite. I feel at peace, and in that calm state of mind, I wonder, why am I doing all of this?

Does any of it make sense? There are so many people who live lives without these fraught relationships, without these crazy hours, without being plagued by ghosts every time they close their eyes.

Maybe there's something else that I could do. Maybe I could just take a break. I deserve it after all, but what would I do for money? What can I even do for a living that isn't detective work?

Without realizing exactly how I got there, I

drive into the parking lot of the police station, park under a towering pine with football-sized cones scattered all around. I pick one up, the prettiest one with the most perfect cone scale and despite the sap that sticks to the edges of my fingertips, I toss it in the front seat of my car.

I don't have an appointment with Captain Carville, and I hope he has time to see me. As soon as he spots me in the hallway through the blinds in his office, he pops his head out and calls me inside. By the tone of his voice and the firing of his eyebrows, I flashback to being called to the principal's office after getting into a fight with a girl in my 4th grade class who stole my graham cracker.

"Have a seat," he barks into the phone, holding the receiver to his landline phone with his shoulder. "I'm going to have to call you back. I've got some urgent business here. I wasn't sure you were going to come in, but thanks for saving me the time and looking for you."

"Yes, of course," I give him a weak smile. "I just wanted to talk to you about Anthony and--"

"No, first, you're going to tell me about your trip to the prison to talk to Victor McFadden."

My heart sinks. How does he know about that?

"I guess you haven't been returning the calls to your friend Special Agent Donald C. Clark because he got a little desperate and reached out to me trying to find you. He said that you went to the prison to talk to McFadden and that you might know something about the case against David Trincia. At least, the case that he's trying to make."

Chapter 30

Captain Carville takes me by surprise. I had no idea that anyone knew about my visit to the prison or my conversation with David besides Donald. I never imagined that he would betray me in that trust.

"You care to tell me about what you two talked about?"

"Why would he tell you?" I blurt out. "I mean, this makes no sense."

"Why don't you mind your own business?" he says. "It's my job to check up on things that are going on in this town and that involves retired FBI agents that have gone rogue and are working outside of their jurisdiction."

"He's entitled to investigate whatever he wants. It's a free country. I mean he could be a journalist doing this."

"Yes, he could, but he's not. He has an agenda. He wants to tie cases that have nothing to do with one another to one ultimate serial killer and to bring attention to the Pacific Northwest as a breeding ground for these things. It's bad enough that we had the Green River Killer, but this would be way worse."

"Is that what this is about?" I ask. "You're worried about public perception?"

"You know that's not entirely it, right?"

"I feel like he's on a wild goose chase, so why do you care so much?" I ask.

"Let's say he is, but there's lots of conspiracy theorists out there saying all sorts of stuff about who killed Kennedy, whether or not we actually went to the moon, all that junk."

"It shouldn't bother you if you don't believe it."

"No, it shouldn't, but it does because he's now contacting LAPD detectives to do his work. Right? Like in your case?"

"It's not like that," I say.

“Then tell me what it’s like.”

“I don't know if I believe what he believes and for a while, I didn't want to go to talk to Victor McFadden in prison. But time was running out, and I figured I have nothing to lose. He put my name on the list, I showed up, they let me in, we had a nice chat."

"And?"

"Victor believes what he's saying. Whether that's the truth is up for debate."

"Are you saying that he's delusional?"

"No, not at all. I'm just saying that that was a close friend of his. His uncle technically, but they grew up together. They were best friends, seemingly. As adults they grew apart a little bit but not much. There were financial differences and his uncle was really affected by how well off Victor had become and there were jealousies with that. But beyond that, I'm unclear. This is all Victor's perception of course and that could be tainted as well. When he told him the story, connecting the three murders, they were on a bender, drinking a lot. He never brought it up again, but that night he told him the locations of three bodies and that the demon was inside of him or after him and he was the one who was responsible for killing those people.

"Victor didn't seem to want to believe that, but when he looked up the locations, they matched the bodies that were found. Now, of course, he could be confessing to a crime that he had nothing to do with. We all know that's a possibility, but he could also be confessing to crimes that he did commit, telling his best friend what he had done. It's hard for me to gauge more without more talks and without getting more involved into who Victor really is, but that's what we talked about."

Captain Carville taps his fingernails on the table. He sips on his oversize mug of coffee, finishing the last bit. He turns around and pops another Keurig into his personal machine right behind him. He's an addict, the way many of us are, because once you find something that alleviates the pressure of the job, you stick to it, and you overdo it until it stops working.

"I'm sorry I didn't tell you. I haven't even talked to Donald yet. I was just trying to figure out my thoughts on it. He asked me for my assessment, and I didn't want to be influenced by what he believes, but I shouldn't have been ignoring his calls. What do you think about this?"

"Well, your conversations with him definitely give Donald's theory a little bit more credibility, but I'm still skeptical. The way that they were killed, the ages and the different types of people that were murdered. None of that adds up. As you know, usually serial killers go after the same type of victim and use the same manner of death."

"Yes. That's what makes this one so hard to solve."

"We all want to believe something," he adds.

We sit in silence with that for a while. The consequences are, of course, dire. If this isn't pursued further, more people will likely die because this man will not stop until he's caught, or dead, or killed.

"I have to talk to you about something else," I say, taking a deep breath. "Cora Leonelle. I need to talk to you about her son."

Anthony seemed to be a sore subject for Captain Carville. He didn't really want to talk about him and his mother's case, but when I kept pressing, he acquiesced.

"To tell you the truth, we're not really anywhere close to figuring out who did it. Her ex-husband and her boyfriend are both suspects. They both have alibis, but the ex-husband's alibi is his current wife. She has a reason to lie, but she's quite reliable."

"Anthony said that his father is very controlling, his stepmother lives under his thumb," I say.

"Is he abusive?" he asks.

"He hasn't said that explicitly, but that doesn't mean that he's not influencing her statements to the police."

"Without evidence of that, we really don't have much to go on."

I sigh deeply and tell him about my concerns, especially those circulating around his father's desire to cremate his ex-wife.

"Anthony's very concerned about the cremation process destroying her body and any possible evidence that can be tested in the future," I say.

"Yes, if I were him, I'd be concerned about that too."

"Is there anything you can do?"

"We can try to delay the approval, but once we've released the body to Cora's next of kin and his guardian, there's not much we can do, unless he goes to court and legally makes himself an adult in order to make decisions as next of kin. Since he's still underage, his father is in charge by proxy."

"That's what I told him," I sigh. "It would require an emergency court order. He has to hire a lawyer now, he has to go through it very quickly, and the likelihood is his father will be very angry and kick him out of the house, not support him in any way."

"Is he willing to deal with that fallout on a maybe?" The Captain asks.

"You seem to be siding with his stepfather"

"Yes, I am. He's innocent until proven guilty. We have no idea that he was at all involved in this, and maybe he has his faults, maybe he could be nicer, but he's his father, and if he didn't kill Anthony's mother, then I don't see any reason why Anthony can't maintain a relationship with him. I butted heads with my dad plenty as a kid, and then things changed when I got older. You go to college, you go away, you get some space. After that, you come back and you can talk more like adults. Your father doesn't nag you about every little thing, treats you more like a man, it happens. You can have good relationships as adults which you didn't have as kids. I see it all the time. Yes, I have a problem with accusing this man of a murder that we don't have any evidence he committed and forcing this court situation, which would undoubtedly create a rift in the family over a maybe, a possibility of evidence to be collected in the future. The medical examiner, the CSI team, they took a lot of fluids, evidence, everything else, so if there are advances in technology in crime scene investigation, we have evidence to test. Maybe it's not as good as a whole body, but it's something."

I give him a slight nod. I can't very well disagree with the reasoning. If Anthony were to take his father to court, it would cause an unnecessary rift. One that he would likely not recover from and he would lose whatever family he has left, a stepmother and siblings. It will be much harder to repair the relationship after getting a court-ordered emancipation. I wouldn't recommend that to any child because things change. Relationships are fluid. The things that you think can never be repaired, can be.

"He's not going to be happy to hear about any of this," I say.

"Yes, and that's why I think maybe you being there or just telling him yourself would be the best way to go."

"I don't know," I shake my head. "I'm not officially on the case after all."

"Yes, but he has reached out to you before, he trusts you. Maybe you can explain this to him. Maybe push him not to automatically consider his father a suspect just because he doesn't seem to give a damn. Because frankly, it's not like they got divorced recently. He's remarried, they've been apart for years. We know of no fights they've had. In fact, their relationship seemed to be better than ever. It was cordial, friendly even."

"Yes, that's true," I say.

"So, what's the motive? Why do it?"

"She had this new boyfriend."

"So what?"

"According to him, he thinks she's an escort. What about that?" I ask.

The Captain offers me another cup of coffee and is working on his third in the time that we've been talking.

"Don't worry, there's plenty of cream and sugar in here to offset the caffeine. I'm actually switching to decaffeinated next week, wish me luck," he adds with a wink.

When he offers to make me a cup, I say no thank you.

"We weren't able to find any evidence of her being an escort," he says definitively. "Theodor seems to think that, but there's nothing on her laptop, no other accounts, no other secret email accounts, phone numbers associated with her account. Nothing. She could have been a super spy, had everything separated and not have any entanglements with her main laptop and iPad and phone, but that seems unlikely."

I have to agree with him. If she had another identity, she would've undoubtedly started another email address that's unassociated with her real name, as well as a burner phone with a new phone number, but the likelihood that we would ever find any pictures or any cross contamination that she is logged into these accounts on her regular laptop or regular iPad just to check up on what's happening seems highly unlikely. She only had one laptop, one iPad, and if she did have two phones, then she was very strict about her usage. I guess that's possible, but who nowadays is that strict? Especially when she wasn't exactly doing something super illegal, she would just want to keep it secret from her son.

"He checked everything," I say. "He checked her iCloud, he checked her other account. He checked even her other social media accounts that showed up from years ago and nothing, no evidence of it whatsoever."

"So why would her ex say that?"

"He could be making it up," I offered. "He could just be disparaging her character. Maybe he couldn't believe the fact that she was making all that money styling and cutting hair."

"She had a lot saved," Captain Carville says. "She lived within her means and she was putting money away. She had a college fund for Anthony, and she had about $300,000 in the bank."

"Wow."

"Yes, and she did make a lot of plans. There were emails back and forth about moving down to Phoenix with her new boyfriend."

"What about him? He could have done it. Just snapped or something."

"He has an ironclad alibi, and you saw him yourself, right? He seems very distraught over what happened."

"Yes," I say. "I hate to say that this might be some stranger because those are the hardest cases to solve, but in this case, it's starting to look like it, doesn't it?"

He gives me a nod, takes another step from his mug. I look at the map of the city behind him, and then follow his gaze out the window at a little crow jumping on the lawn outside.

"I'm going to be leaving tomorrow," I say.

"Keep me updated if there're any breakthroughs in the case and let me know if you want me to call Anthony and try to talk to him about the cremation. Talk him into keeping things cordial with his father, despite the cremation conversation. Who knows, maybe his father will agree to let him use some of that money he is going to inherit for the burial."

"Perhaps," Captain Carville says with a nod, flashing a smile. "I thank you for the visit, but I'm not exactly a fan of the circumstances under which we met."

"Yes, I'm sorry about that. I don't usually make it a habit of going on trips and finding dead bodies. It just sort of happened that way."

"Well, it was nice to meet you, Kaitlyn. You stay in touch now."

I leave the station with all of my questions unanswered, but at peace, nevertheless. There's no explanation for it, except that that's just how it is with certain cases. You just don't know, and perhaps, you never will.

31

The Night Of The Disappearance

Cora had plans to meet with Steven in only five minutes. She was so excited that she could hardly contain herself. She wanted to get to the curb and wait there. Everything was set. The lights were turned off, the door was locked. Another day at the salon was over, but her life was only just beginning. She'd had Anthony young, and Steven didn't seem to want any kids. At least they hadn't talked about it much. He still couldn't believe that he could retire so early, but he was waiting around for Anthony to graduate so that she would go with him. After years of being alone and prior to that, years of being with a man who tried to control her every move and who never had anything nice or polite to say to her, she couldn't believe her luck.

Part of her was sad that she had wasted time not dating him, putting him in the friend zone because she was afraid. But she was making up for it now, and starting today was better than waiting until tomorrow.

She usually wore her hair up at work to not have it get in her face while she colored and cut other people's locks. But for this date, she let it fall over her shoulders. The cool highlights and the extra waves that were augmented by perfectly placed extensions that added a volume and panache that she greatly appreciated. She was wearing size two jeans, a short crop top and boots. Big turquoise earrings to draw attention to her eyes and her favorite red cross-body bag with the locket inside which she still needed to get fixed.

"Today's going to be the day when everything changes," she told herself. "Anthony would know the truth. I will stop hiding."

She was almost giddy at what the future held. She still couldn't believe that Steven had saved up enough money for a retirement and that Southern California or Phoenix or somewhere warm in the Sunbelt was waiting for them.

She wasn't entirely sure how Anthony would react, but he had plans for the south as well, the beaches or the desert. He was applying to moderately priced schools, and with a straight A average and his participation in all the clubs and volunteer opportunities she was certain that he stood a good chance of getting in wherever he chose. She had even tried to encourage him to apply to some Ivy League Schools or at least the top twenty colleges in the nation. But he wanted a scholarship, and so if his grades were better for a lower-tier school and it was more affordable, that's what he wanted to do. Anthony was smart that way.

She stood outside waiting. The street was dark. The light had just gone off and she hadn't noticed how dark it was because, well, she rarely stood out here after closing. For some reason she decided to tonight. She wanted to see Steven when he first pulled up. She didn't want to bother with him parking or anything like that.

She wanted to hop into his car and head toward her house, toward the truth, toward her new future. The last thing she expected at that moment was a leather-gloved hand to wrap its hard fingers around her mouth so that she couldn't move and for the barrel of a gun to be pressed into her ribcage.

She winced in pain and shock, and her heart started to beat out of her chest for an entirely different reason.

"What are you doing?" she tried to mumble. "Who are you?" but no words came out.

"Shut up," he said and reached into her phone pocket almost as if he knew exactly where she had put her keys.

Had he been watching her? Her heart skipped a beat.

The man opened the door to the dark salon, pushed her inside almost throwing her onto one of the chairs. Cora was about to open her mouth when he threatened, "Don't say a word or I'll shoot you. I've done it before."

She did as she was told.

"What do you want? Take whatever's in the cash register."

It suddenly occurred to her that maybe he was just a burglar. In the shadows, she could see the ski mask, the broad shoulders, the wide stance. He was probably a middle-aged male, white based on his voice, but even that she wasn't sure about.

He had artificially lowered it to sound different. She couldn't see his face because a black ski mask covered it all except for the flickering of the eyes at steady intervals. Nothing about him was rushed. His hands were covered in black leather gloves. He wore dark pants and a dark jacket.

"What do you want?" she asked.

"You," he rasped.

Her whole life flashed before her eyes: holding Anthony as a baby in her hands for the first time, taking him to preschool, first grade, eighth grade graduation, the highs and lows, mostly the highs; her toxic divorce. Her controlling ex-husband didn't make much of a blip, but Steven did.

Steven who was coming soon. Should she tell this armed intruder who had pressed what look to be a silencer into her forehead, should she tell him that he was coming?

That he was going to be here any moment? She wasn't sure if that would make it worse? What if she said something, and then he took Steven hostage too?

No, it's better that it would just be her, but what if Steven could help? A million thoughts rushed through her mind all at once.

Slowly, at the same time, her breath quickened and then relaxed, and then suddenly, there was a knock at the door.

"You say a word and you're dead, and so is your friend over there," the man pressed the silencer into her skin.

Did he know that she was expecting someone? Did he follow her? For how long?

“Cora?" Steven's voice sounded muffled through the thick glass.

She had splurged for the more expensive kind that would allow her to play music louder for her customers if they were having a party or special get-together at the salon.

Cora didn't want to bother the neighbors, but now she hated that decision. What she wouldn’t have done to go back to that moment and change it all.

Steven continued to knock. He didn't give up easily, and then her phone rang. The man took it from her and turned it off.

"We're going to wait for your friend to leave. If you make a sound, you and he are both dead."

"What do you want?" Cora whispered.

She couldn't see much, but she thought that he had narrowed his eyes.

Steven called again and again. The masked man pressed the button to ignore. If you made enough calls, you knew when the call went to voicemail and when it was ignored.

The man was doing this to send a signal to Steven to leave. It's almost as if she, Cora, was telling him to go.

She watched his shadow through the window. He hesitated for a while, walked back and forth, texted her, and then got back into his car and took off.

She wanted to scream and yell for him, but she wanted him to live. She couldn't imagine watching him be part of this, whatever was going to happen. It was only going to happen to her.

Cora kept quiet to protect Steven, to save him because, perhaps, a part of her knew that this was the end.

She didn't dare let herself think that, but how could she not? A man was pointing a gun in her face, holding her hostage.

Still, something deep inside of Cora told her that she had to fight. The end can come so quickly and without a battle. She wouldn't just let him take her, and not stand up for her life.

Cora searched the room. He had deadbolted the front door, so if she were to run for it, she'd have to grab onto the lock first, turn it, swing the door open and escape, but for that, she would need to buy time. She needed to hurt him. Incapacitate him.

"Why are you doing this?" She asked to hear the answer, but also to buy herself some time. "You don't have to hurt me. If you want to take anything here, go ahead."

"I'm not here for money," The man said with a smirk. "And I'm not here because I want to be. Know that, okay?" He seemed almost sorry for a moment, like he was being forced to do something against his will.

"What are you talking about?" She asked. "You don't have to do any of this if you don't want to."

"If it was only so easy."

Her chest tightened Was there somebody else who was going to take her? Someone else who was threatening him?

Chapter 32

The man walked around in front of Cora, pacing back and forth. He had a casual gait about him, the way that a man would walk doing gardening around his house, and yet Cora saw something that resembled a nervousness in him. He peeked a little bit at his fingers.

Was that hesitation? Cora sensed in the dark, even though her eyes had adjusted. She was careful in her movements. She kept her body rigid but moved her hand slightly back.

There was a drawer at the bottom that she knew that she could reach where she had kept her old scissors. These were the ones that didn't work as well, ones she kept just in case someone had borrowed her good pair.

She knew that the drawer might squeak, but if

she pulled it out just so, it wouldn't. She wrapped her whole hand around it. Luckily, it was rather slim, and instead of pulling the handle, she pulled it out slightly holding the entire drawer in between her thumb and the edges of her fingertips.

The man's face was turned away, but he kept his gun pointed at her. Cora picked up the scissors slowly, wrapped her hand around them and held her breath as she pushed the drawer back in, wondering if this was even worth the effort in case she got caught. But he didn't seem to be paying attention, at least not to this part.

Steven was long gone. He knocked a little bit longer, called her phone, texted, but after peering into the darkness, he had probably assumed that there had been a change of plans. Maybe she couldn't tell him about it quite yet. As much as she prayed for him to go away, she now wished that he would come back and rescue her.

On one of those TV shows, somewhere, she heard that if someone takes you like this, you should keep talking. Especially if they don't kill you right away, you should keep talking humanize yourself, to build up sympathy for who you are as a person. Initially, you were a stranger, someone to be taken, kidnapped, maybe killed, but perhaps with a little bit of conversation, you could be much harder to ignore, much harder to simply throw away and discard like trash.

“I'm a mother. My son, he wants to go to school in California. He wants to get away from the rain. Do you like the rain?” she asked, not certain where else to start figuring that the weather is perhaps as good a spot as any.

"What are you doing?" he said. "Why are you talking to me?"

"It's just the two of us here. You have a gun pointed at my head. What do you want?"

"I want that guy out there to leave and make sure that he's gone for good."

"Okay, seems like he is." Cora said. "What now? I don't think you want to do this. I think you want--"

"You don't know anything about me," he snapped.

"Okay. So, tell me, I'm going to listen."

"No," he paced again.

Cora realized that talking to him was making him nervous, and she didn't know why. She wrapped her fingers tightly around the scissors as if they were a knife.

If I use this correctly, it's going to be a good weapon, she said to herself silently, but it's the element of surprise that's going to get him.

"Tell me why you're doing this," she started to say but then he pressed his hand over her mouth, pushing an awful smelling piece of fabric inside and over her nose.

"No," she mumbled.

The fumes rushed through her, and darkness wrapped around her.

Cora didn't know where she was or what she was doing here. The only thing she knew was that she was in a cabin. The scent of wet pine permeated throughout. She had a pounding headache from whatever she had been drugged with. She found herself tied to the metal stove with rope. Her arms were behind her. The scissors were long gone, and she was lying on her side in the fetal position. When she woke up, she managed to sit up, but she couldn't sit too close to the stove because it was hot to the touch.

The man who'd taken her was snoring on the couch, illuminated by the fire, still wearing the ski mask over his head. Does that mean that he may want to let her go, or did he just forget?

There are empty bottles of beer and a liter of cheap vodka sitting on the coffee table. His snores are loud, but the cabin is small, low ceiling, one room, not even a bed, just the couch right there and a table in the back. It didn't seem like something that you would use for an overnight. His snores filled the entire cabin. He slept for a long time, so long that Cora ended up closing her eyes and lowering herself to sleep as well.

She lay back down on the floor, her headache thumping, the heat from the stove making her sweat and drenching the back of her shirt. She closed her eyes and tried to think of a way to get out of there.

Sometime later that night, she heard him wake up, walk around the cabin, muttering to himself. She pretended to be asleep and listened with her eyes open just enough to peer through her eyelashes at him.

There was one small light on the dining room table, and nothing else but the fire that was starting to fizzle out. He put another log on it, continuing to mutter to himself. The way he walked, it was obvious he was drunk.

At first, Cora couldn't make out what he was saying.

It's almost as If he were talking to her, though.

"You asked me why I'm doing this. Not because I want to, that's for sure."

He growls. "I wouldn't be doing this. You think I'm doing this because I love it? I get some sick pleasure from it? No, I have to. I have no choice."

Cora was not sure if he was talking *to* her or *at* her, but she kept quiet. She didn't want him to know that she was awake.

"Don't you understand?" he said, throwing some kindling on the fire. "Don't you understand I didn't want to do any of them, but *he* made me do it. It's the demon," he said, "I have to. If I don't, he won't leave me alone."

Their eyes met for a moment. He saw her listening.

“Please don’t," Cora said sitting up, the illusion of being asleep vanishing.

"Otherwise he won't leave me alone,” he mumbled. “He’ll haunt me in my sleep, and during the days, he'll come around as well and be here all the time. Do you know what that's like, to always have someone watching you, waiting for you to do what he says?"

"What is he telling you to do?"

"To kill."

"Please, sir, no," Cora’s voice cracked. "I have a son. I have a family. Don't you have people who love you?"

"I did." He laughed.

He was moving in and out of lucidity, in and out of his drunken state. Sometimes he seemed perfectly clear, and other times his eyes flickered with insanity.

"Sir, please, you can still fix this. Just take me back and I won't call the police, nothing."

"I don't care about the police."

He grabbed a hold of the back of her hands. He untied one part that was attached to the stove and started to pull her out toward the front door. She tried to kick whatever she could, kick him, kick at the ground, but he continued to pull. He was much stronger than he looked. He still wore the mask.

Why? Why didn't he want her to see who he was? She continued to fight, but he pulled on her arms just so, and the torsion made it feel like they were about to break.

"Some people will look for you and then others will just forget. That's how it works."

"You don't have to do this," Cora screamed. "You don't have to do this."

"Are you going to take care of that demon? He's the one that's making me kill you. He's the one that wants blood. He says over and over again. I don't want to do this."

"You don't have to," she pleaded.

For a moment, he hesitated, and Cora could see a bit of humanity in him, but then it was like a film came over his eyes and everything changed.

He put on his gloves. She scrambled to her feet to run. She managed to get about ten feet when he caught up to her.

He hit her over the head with something, and when she came back to he was on top of her, his gloved hand covering her mouth and nose, and the other pressing down on her windpipe. Cora struggled to breathe, and she continued to fight until a few minutes later when it became easier to just let go.

33

Today

The day is light gray. Being in the Pacific Northwest this long, I've started to distinguish among the various shades. It's not exactly overcast full of rain, but not particularly welcoming either. Darkness is looming all around, even though it's not even noon yet.

We had breakfast in an old diner that looks like it was on its way out, ripped seats, dirty windows, but the food came out tasting so delicious, with just the right amount of sugar and fat, that it was probably the best thing I've had in a long time.

Our flight is not until later that night, and we have the majority of the day to kill. I suggest we go sightseeing, but Luke has a better idea. We head down to check out David Trincia's house. It's completely on a whim with no real reason to go, except that we know that he will be at work and we might get a good look around.

This is nothing that we run by Donald, who is finally on the cruise with his wife. We had briefly spoken about my meeting with Viktor and he had just received good news from his oncologist about his levels improving and the possibility of his cancer going into remission in the future. I wished him a good trip and promised to call when I got home.

"What do you want to do?" I ask when we pull up to the quaint, modest two-bedroom in a working-class community of Portland, Oregon. If David Trincia has money, he lives within his means.

The house isn't exactly in shambles, but it's not pristine either. In some parts, it is well taken care of. In others, it is completely ignored. Perhaps the repainting job is being done in sections. The neighbors who were on their porches before are now gone. And as far as I can tell, there are no cameras around.

Getting out of the car, Luke spots the for-sale sign swinging in the breeze.

"Perfect," he says with a wink. "We can be a couple checking out the community. If we happen to look into the neighbor's yards, then so be it."

"I hope this is not what you're like at work." I

say jokingly. "None of your searches would stand up in court."

"Oh, we don't need a warrant to walk around."

Being here in his front yard makes me a little bit uncomfortable. If David Trincia is actually the murderer and he spots us nosing around, it will put him on alert. But it's too late to second guess this decision. We're already here.

Admiring the trim around the windows, I use that as an excuse to step closer to the glass for a better peek.

I walk confidently around the place, looking at the tree, the outside of the house, all to appear as if I'm only here inspecting the surroundings. When I get brave enough, I peek in through the windows. First, the two front windows, and then I wander all the way to the gate.

The side windows faced the living room. When I peeked in there wasn't anything too out of place. A used, sunken-in couch, a newer chair, a nondescript coffee table probably made from some compressed wood material, just like mine.

Then for some reason, I glance back once at Luke, and open the latch to the gate, to the fence.

"What are you doing?" he hissed in my direction.

"I'm just going to go look at this tree back here," I say still playing the part of a prospective home buyer. "It's so beautiful!" I add with great exaggeration.

I don't bother closing the gate because the prospective home buyer wouldn't. I'm not hiding the fact that I'm here. In fact, quite the opposite. I'm demonstratively looking.

As soon as I am behind the house, out of sight, I peek into the windows in the back, these face the bedroom. There is a queen size bed in the corner. Sheets, a dark green color and unmade with limp pillows stacked flatly against the mattress.

Across from it is a dresser cluttered with junk, including empty bottles of beer, books, even a typewriter, and then something catches my eye.

It's peeking out from the second drawer from the top. The drawer itself is pulled out just a little bit. I see the strap and part of a red cross-body bag.

I pull on my phone and stare at the screenshot that Anthony had sent me of the exact bag that his mother had purchased at TJ Maxx. Cora had spent almost $70 on it which, for her, was a stretch. It was a gift to herself, not the kind she got very often.

Could this be it?

For a second I wonder if my eyes are betraying me.

I lean back wanting to yell for Luke, but not wanting to draw any attention.

I take out my phone and luckily the light is just right for me to zoom in and take a picture of it. It looks exactly like it.

The strap is made partly of red felt material and partly of the chain just like in Anthony's picture.

There's a small possibility that David Trincia could have bought the same bag himself, but it seems so out of place here in this house.

There's not a single other thing that would say a woman was here, and yet here is this bag. But how could it be? Where was *he* when Cora was killed? Where was he when those three other bodies that I know of were murdered?

A cold sweat runs down my back as I slowly step away from the window and rush back to Luke. I tell him about the purse and urge him to look himself while I act as the lookout.

I pace with a grim smile on my face, looking at the trees and the craftsman architecture of the neighborhood all the while my heart pounding is inside.

When Luke returns, his face is pale white. All blood seemed to have somehow drained from it. He stares at me with his distracted eyes and gives me a nod.

"It definitely looks like it," he says slowly and

deliberately, uncertain of his words. "But we can't go in there."

I already know that. We have no warrant. If we break in then this piece of evidence gets tossed out. We shouldn't have even been looking in the back window since the gate was closed but that little bit, no one has to know.

"Let's get out of here before someone sees us," I say, quietly.

As we drive away, we both know that everything is different now. We can't go back home, not quite yet.

We have to find out if that is Cora's purse in David Trincia's bedroom.

We have to find out if David Trincia is the one responsible for her death…

Thank you for reading. Want to find out what happens next as Kaitlyn's hunt for the serial killer continues as she looks deeper into the mysteries surrounding her father's death? **1-click Girl Hunted (Girl Missing Book 7) now!**

Kaitlyn Carr's hunt for the serial killer continues as she delves deeper into the mysteries surrounding her father's death.

After receiving a letter from a retired FBI

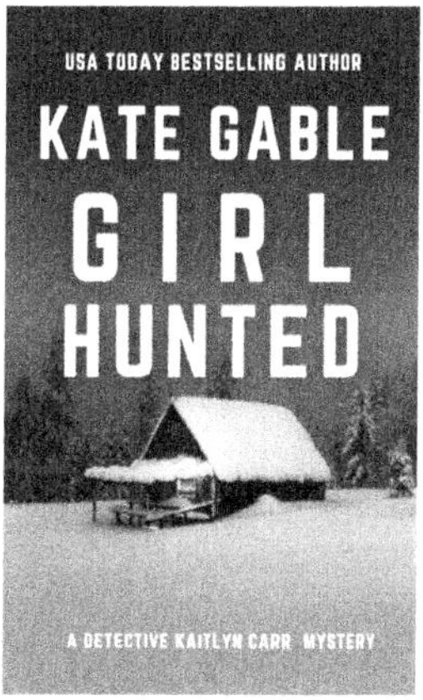

agent, Kaitlyn's world is turned upside down once again. The letter claims that her father's death was not an accident, but a murder. In order to uncover the truth, Kaitlyn and her boyfriend, FBI Agent Luke Galvinson, must help the agent solve a series of cold cases that he believes are connected to the same illusive serial killer.

As Kaitlyn investigates the cold cases, she finds herself in a secluded cabin in the woods where her life is endangered. This is the perfect place for the killer to hide their victims. Kaitlyn wonders if she is getting closer to the killer or if it's the other way around. She finds herself questioning everything, from her own investigation to the people she thought she could trust.

In this seventh installment of the Girl Missing series, Kaitlyn's hunt for the serial killer takes her to the Pacific Northwest, a place with a near-constant cover of clouds and rain. It's a place where the beauty of nature is juxtaposed with the darkness of the killer's deeds. Kaitlyn finds herself facing a killer who is always one step ahead of her and who seems to know her every move.

With twists and turns at every corner, Gone Forever will keep you on the edge of your seat until the very end. It's the perfect addition to the Girl Missing series and a must-read for fans of James Patterson, AJ Rivers and Karin Slaughter.

Join Kaitlyn Carr on her quest for justice and the truth about her father's death. Get your copy of Gone Forever now and find out what happens in this heart-pounding thriller.

1-click Girl Hunted (Girl Missing Book 7) now!

Can't get enough of Kaitlyn Carr? Read the **Girl Hidden (FREE Novella) now!**

Be the first to know about
my upcoming sales, new
releases and exclusive
giveaways!

Want a Free book? Sign up for my Newsletter!

Sign up for my newsletter:
https://www.subscribepage.com/kategableviplist

Join my Facebook Group: https://www.facebook.com/groups/833851020557518

Bonus Points: Follow me on BookBub and Goodreads!

https://www.goodreads.com/author/show/21534224.Kate_Gable

About Kate Gable

Kate Gable loves a good mystery that is full of suspense. She grew up devouring psychological thrillers and crime novels as well as movies, tv shows and true crime.

Her favorite stories are the ones that are centered on families with lots of secrets and lies as well as many twists and turns. Her novels have elements of psychological suspense, thriller, mystery and romance.

Kate Gable lives near Palm Springs, CA with her husband, son, a dog and a cat. She has spent more than twenty years in Southern California and finds inspiration from its cities, canyons, deserts, and small mountain towns.

She graduated from University of Southern California with a Bachelor's degree in Mathematics. After pursuing graduate studies in mathematics, she switched gears and got her MA in Creative Writing and English from Western New Mexico University and her PhD in Education from Old Dominion University.

Writing has always been her passion and

obsession. Kate is also a USA Today Bestselling author of romantic suspense under another pen name.

Write her here:

Kate@kategable.com

Check out her books here:

www.kategable.com

Sign up for my newsletter:

https://www.subscribepage.com/kategableviplist

Join my Facebook Group:

https://www.facebook.com/groups/833851020557518

Bonus Points: Follow me on BookBub and Goodreads!

https://www.bookbub.com/authors/kate-gable

https://www.goodreads.com/author/show/21534224.Kate_Gable

amazon.com/Kate-Gable/e/B095XFCLL7

facebook.com/kategablebooks

bookbub.com/authors/kate-gable

instagram.com/kategablebooks

Also by Kate Gable

Detective Kaitlyn Carr Psychological Mystery series

Girl Missing (Book 1)

Girl Lost (Book 2)

Girl Found (Book 3)

Girl Taken (Book 4)

Girl Forgotten (Book 5)

Girl Deceived (Book 6)

Girl Hunted (Book 7)

Girl Shadowed (Book 8)

Girl Hidden (FREE Novella)

FBI Agent Alexis Forrest Series

Forest of Silence

Forest of Shadows

Forest of Secrets

Forest of Lies
Forest of Obsession
Forest of Regrets

Detective Charlotte Pierce Psychological Mystery series
Last Breath
Nameless Girl
Missing Lives
Girl in the Lake

Lake of Lies (FREE Novella)

Printed in Great Britain
by Amazon

58500381R00169

MIKE MELDRUM

THE DEADLY SINS OF LEADERSHIP

This edition first published in paperback by
Michael Terence Publishing in 2025
www.mtp.agency

ISBN 9781805880387

Cover illustration
by Warren FitzGerald

Michael Terence
Publishing